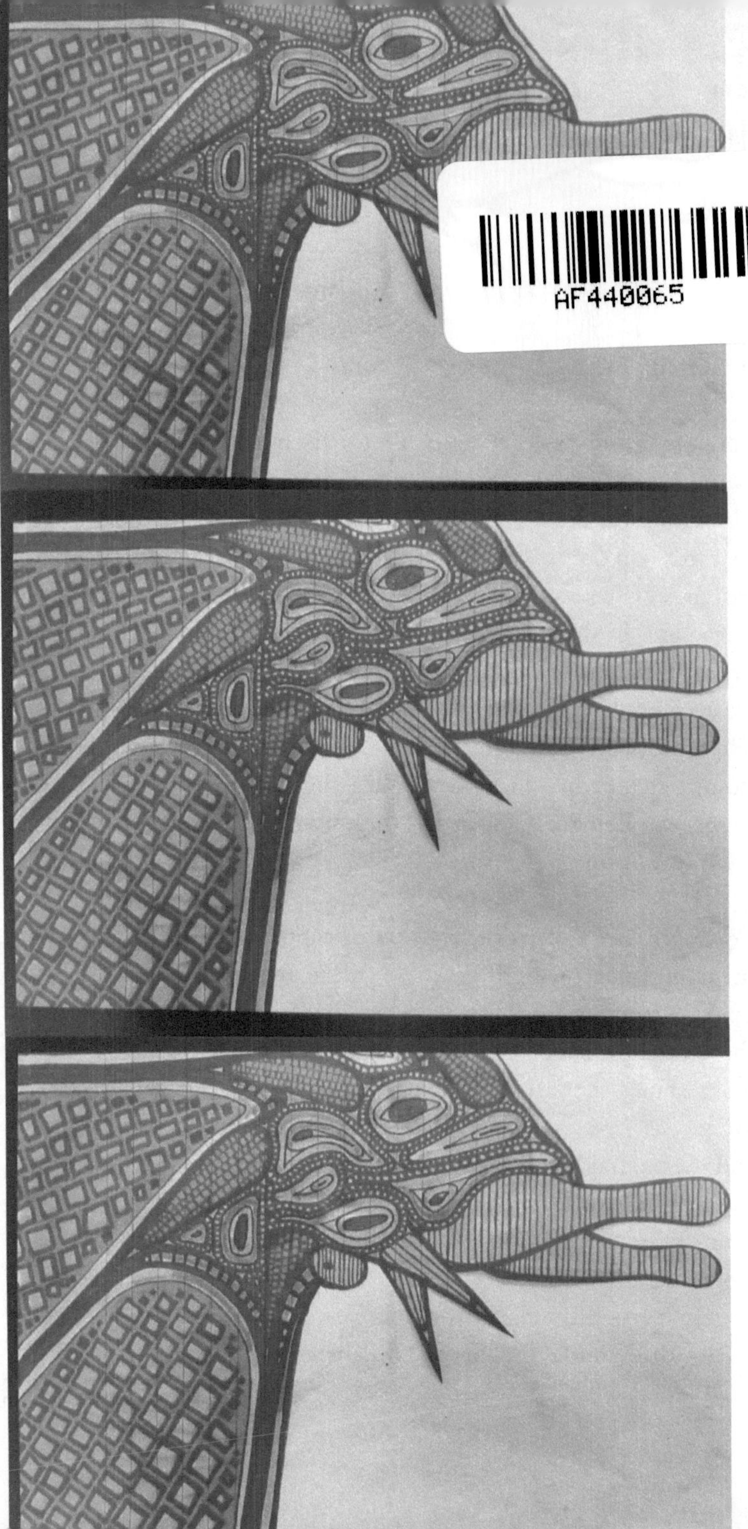
AF440065

The fresh, previously unheard notes in Ben Segal's brain-feverish surrealism arrive in the reader's mind with an audaciously hypercompact lyricism, and his sentences dart straight to the heart. *Pool Party Trap Loop*'s expertly miniaturized fictions of bodily havoc, of messily human collision, introduce Ben Segal as a vital and original voice.
**– Garielle Lutz**

Suppose every fable is tired. One's been the child painter for years. Another the Worm King for every dream. Over there is the girl who can't drown. Down in the vacuum are the people living by cards. Up on the Ferris wheel is the wrestler in a red signet that matches his beard. In the end it's all another legacy, another trial, a true life. In this mischievously enchanting collection, Ben Segal knows that tinsel rusts, and that's when things get real-hearted. A clear-colored sadness leaks from real bodies and philosophies. The ghosts are here, but they live in buckets. The squirrels are dead, but they live in jackets. What they all sing for is to be at peace, and Ben Segal gets it all on spools of fugue.
**– Mike Young**

*Pool Party Trap Loop* is a collection of captivating stories sheathed in grammatical glitz. In each of these narrative nuggets Segal exploits form and conceit while simultaneously tightrope walking the excitingly dangerous arena of the artful sentence.... Segal's work stands alone in its strange, winding, sudden candor. *Pool Party Trap Loop* is a collection for the intellectually adventurous and the unafraid. The sentence level beauty and large-scale conceit ingenuity make it a serious read that requires, between stories, even more serious pause. Reading *Pool Party Trap Loop* is wounding to the memory – it's a collection that will pull you in, swirl you around, and spit you out mangled and changed.
**– Rita Bullwinkle**, Full Stop Magazine

The stories that Segal writes reflect each other, sometimes in mirrored pairs. But where palindromes create an illusion of order by deforming words, Segal assembles elegant words to evoke a fucked up reality. More than anything, Ben Segal reminds me of a young Raymond Queneau. Except he's not French. And he's alive.

– **Michael Vegas Mussman**, Pank Magazine

*Pool Party Trap Loop* is a palindrome and a nightmare. … I, a mere outsider looking in, would classify this as a book that is far more about traps and loops than pools or parties. Perhaps pools and parties enter the equation from time to time, but this is a book devoted to the lure, to the art of ensnarement, with body horror its most frequent loop….[Segal] has created a dazzling world.

– **Carolyn DeCarlo**, Heavy Feather Review

If the stories in *Pool Party Trap Loop* are a full-frontal attack – which I believe they are – the attack is not on the reader, but rather on the larger constructs that affect the way we fuck and think and speak. Its purpose is to remind us that language, sex, violence, and even issues of conduct are inescapable and intractable, the only thing worth acknowledging, deserving of both our respect and contempt. If surrealism seems to suggest freedom and liberation, Ben's work conversely demonstrates a series of structures – ethical, societal, linguistic – crashing into each other in ways that may be shocking, but make complete and absolute sense when set against the lattice of rules that govern and fragment our daily lives.

– **Keith McCleary**, Electric Literature

Published in 2022 by

# Schism Neuronics

First edition Queen's Ferry Press, 2015

ISBN: 9798353570592



Printed in London, UK

# POOL PARTY TRAP LOOP

Ben Segal

# Table of Contents

# POOL PARTY

# TRAP LOOP

# WINDOW/SCREENS

A building exists also in language. This one, constructed underground, all glass and black-metal struts, it conjures terms like *cantilevered*. As in: *Why can't he leave her?* It doesn't seem impossible. The windows still swing open; the doors are all in working order.

On the other hand, there are the trappings of modern plumbing: flush toilets and hot showers, sprinkler systems. All kinds of watery enticement.

Mostly there is a jut of ceiling glass, exposed to the sky but level with the earth and so placed as to be a glass panel in an otherwise concrete sidewalk. He watches the obvious things from under—skirt openings, sneaker treads. He likes especially when a bird sets down or shits on the pane from above. He likes the backlit splatter.

—

And what of the stayed-with *her*? She is largely an excuse he furnishes, a projected obstruction to explain his staying in. I.e. *She's not just my ball and chain; she's got my balls enchained.* In fact, she's got more concern for the television. She wears a brownwool hood, an ex-presidential mask, calfskin gloves. She and the others work under the sign of the Dutch boot, nightly saboteurs of broadcast towers.

—

He has fallen deeply in love with his massage chair but sometimes he cheats with his bidet.

Years back, he kept pigeons on a high roof. He met with friends to enjoy their company. His interest in his wife extended beyond agoraphobic utility.



He is this evening in the leather massage chair, undressed, watching the spread of dog piss on his sidewalk skylight. It goes in tentacles. He likes liquid things. His wife has telephoned already, sweetly to inform him that she'll not be home until after he goes to sleep.

Other telephone calls come from former friends. It's a night they would once have gathered on. His ex-friends still do. They would like him to come. He is, they agree, understatedly charming, the best kind of talker. He begs off for various marital priorities: sink leak repair, promised fine dinner, irrational demands stemming from a certain time of the month.

His former friends wonder if 'time of the month' is really a euphemism or just a conveniently vague truth, as time is always, in fact, encased in one month or another.



His wife, with two partners and a driver, has just knocked out the signal from the local NBC station of a middling, nearby hill-bound community. They struck during the weather. Viewers thought maybe they were experiencing an eclipse. The wife and her fellow saboteurs change clothes in the back of their escaping van. They put on matching sweat suits, casual off-yellow drapings of new-money suede and terry cloth, then pile into a chain diner for celebratory dessert.

Some three dogs are peeing with regularity on the roof of the house. The man has been enjoying the territorial competition. It's a kind of endless, victorless sport. He has the massage chair set to *percussion* and is jolting contentedly beneath the urine spread.

———

He does leave the house sometimes; that's a necessary minimum for employment and he's in need of a salary.

A house like his requires payments. The Sharper Image is a far cry from a charity shop.

In lieu of a more desirable sinecure, he has secured himself a position as a functionary. He mostly assesses and sorts, though there is also the occasional bout of filing. The office others are aware of his smile, his many charming teeth. One such other, a managerial figure, some nominally higher-up, at nights re-chews the man's discarded whitening gum.

The re-chewer doesn't realize that the plucked gum wads leave residue ghosts on the garbage bin's sides, that the man's trashcan has become a surveillance device.

———

The man's wife engages also in slow and office-based usefulness. Because she is a radical or terrorist, she is very good at her job.

She plans to be at her office in the morning, poorly rested but with a bright perfected face, a face caked smooth with fine and beautifying powder. Now she is sharing pie and vanilla ice cream. She and the others are laughing. The driver keeps asking their waitress to change the channel to NBC, to just try again. He keeps saying his show is on.

The four companions watch the television's blackness. All there is is dead air; not even a test pattern.

—

At home, her husband has switched from *percussion* to *rolling pressure*. At night the darkness makes his ceiling window hard to watch. There's not usually anything to see anyway. Nights in his neighborhood tend to be empty.

—

Once a woman, a friend of his wife's, had stood spread-legged over his sidewalk window and shot straight down at his face. This was a birthday present. The glass is bulletproof, though the bullets were plenty real. The sound of it was loud, he remembered, and thrilling. The woman's leg had been gouged by the ricocheting rounds and she'd dropped blood on the glass pane and then down along the sidewalk.

—

This night he is staring up, watching for something striking, an instant of a chase maybe, or some act of violence in mid-commission. He would like to be swept up in something terrifying and totally beyond him. He finds romance in the thought of bearing witness. Tonight he sees nothing. The street above his head is calm and the shadows are without portent.

—

His wife comes home just after three. She folds her hood and gloves and slips her mask back into the costume drawer. She can hear the massage chair droning in its steady work. Her husband is sunken into it, sleeping. He is having a wonderful dream about affixing dollar bills to the clear underside of the sidewalk. The dreamed hands of dreamed children slam into the glass. Rebuffed and confused, the children gather to dig for the bills with hopeless vigor. The glass doesn't suffer a scratch.

His wife unplugs the chair and coaxes his mostly sleeping body into bed. They lie, apart, beside each other, yards deep in the earth. Tomorrow is a school day. They'll be woken too early by the footsteps of real children overhead.

# GUMBOY

*Gumboy Goes to School*

A boy who never grew teeth, walking lakefront, harvesting denture stones. He kneads them into his gums.

They set for the day in his drying blood, wash away with his saliva.

School time they come crumbling out, some punctuation, mid-sentence pebbles.

He talks lispedly and high-pitched and only when called on. Stone dust mixes to sludge in his mouth, a gray slurry that dribbles out from his odd-set, grinding jaw.

By night he's down to gums again, red and empty, all wet flesh. He doesn't talk at all then. He walks the lake, pocketing tomorrow's teeth.

*Gumboy Fights the Police*

Pulling small rocks from his mouth, hurling them at a squad car. He's killed a pigeon this way. He unloads everything. The car's pocked lightly now, a little speckled. A thumb, an officer's, dry and rough, runs the length of the boy's gums. They're almost as firm as expected. The officer's hand feels safe. The boy begins to lick and tickle in anger. He curls a finger into the officer's mustache, keeps it moving to the rim of the man's nostril to gently trace its oblique circumference.

No one files a report.

*Gumboy Plays in the Cold*

His mouth's a lump of chattering stone. Flecks of rock and spittle—he's gashing himself up with his shivers.

A kindly vendor offers him hot cocoa, fresh-made, free of charge. The boy drinks gratefully, swallows a stone, chokes and coughs it into the vendor's stall. Cocoa sprays a brown patina on man and his wares. The boy sinks to the snow in shame.

He lines his mouth with snow for penance or the whiteness of it. The vendor stares quietly, begins to wipe himself off.

*Gumboy Meets a Rescue Dog*

Going rockless today, he parts his lips at passing dogs. The dogs seem pleased at the sight.

The boy shakes paws with a beautiful one, a Saint Bernard. The boy pets the dog. He hums at him gently.

With petting, the dog's shed fur builds up between the boy's fingers. He contemplates the stringy mesh. The dog pants slobber, well-content. The dog saves skiers on mountains.

The boy is thinking of whales, how they sift krill through their string teeth. He is dreaming of baleen.

The dog is whistled off to some avalanche or catastrophe, so the boy is left alone with his handful of fur. He presses it between his lips and gumline, breathes in the heavy smell of Saint Bernard. His is a happy baleen day! The thickly choking teeth-net grows damp in the fog of exhalation.

*Gumboy Races a Diplomat*

The boy is sucking the stones in his mouth. Lake lozenges. He has grown too thin, bony-chested, his elbows the widest parts of his arms.

He is walking the city, hungry but without real purpose. A few consular employees linger in front of the Japanese embassy. The boy approaches a lanky bureaucrat and steals the man's sandwich. At first the diplomat is confused. The boy continues walking and begins to eat; the diplomat shouts after him. The boy does not respond.

A careful eater by necessity, the boy breaks a chunk of bread and holds it in his mouth until it sogs to a creamed soup texture. His makeshift teeth are no good at tearing and are pried loose easily in the effort. Instead he rolls his stones over the wetted bread in the hollow of his mouth to better mash each bite into the desired state of slop

The diplomat shouts after the boy once more and is again ignored. He begins to run after the boy, who in turn begins to run as well. The two continue, pursuer and pursued, for many blocks. They pass the piers and keep running, by this point simply for the joy of it, along the loading docks, then back into the neighborhoods. The diplomat catches up to and passes the boy. He raises his arms in triumph. He is smiling. The runners shake each other's hands.

*Gumboy Attends a Funeral*

Weeping, mostly. Most people here are weeping. The casket is open, the same song plays on a loop.

The boy watches it all, mouth shut, unnoticed.

*Gumboy Dies*

His heart stops, his lungs.

The doctor shocks his body to restart it. The boy begins to breathe again. Loosed stones tumble down his throat and he coughs them up, out and into the doctor's hands. The boy collects his stones, stands and bows, then walks away.

# I WOULD KISS HIM BACK
# ALL OVER TOO

(1)

Thylacines, known also as Tasmanian tigers, were striped canids native to the Australian island of Tasmania. They were short and wiry, nearly wolves, distinctively striped from mid-torso to tail.

(2)

Monica loves Chris. The newspaper says she is missing, that she was last seen and where and by whom. There is no ransom note, so Monica is likely either in a fugue state or dead.

(3)

Thylacines were not actually canids. They belonged to a completely unique family of marsupials. Their jaws opened back almost to their eyes and they hunted in the island's low trees.

(4)

If Monica is wandering in a fugue state, she is not Monica but a kind of ghost. If Monica is dead but not known dead, she is a kind of ghost. Therefore Monica is a ghost. Monica is a kind of ghost or a ghost. The newspaper does not say which.

(5)

Though sightings persist, the thylacine is believed to have gone extinct in the 1930s. I like to watch videos of the last known thylacine opening its jaw and pacing about its little concrete cage in the Sydney Zoo.

(6)

Things that you see that are dead are what are ghosts. When these things are captured and are not dead, they are thereby unghosted. If these things are captured and are dead, they are also unghosted. They are then unghosted unless they are seen moving later. That is, if something is seen moving but has a dead and unmoving body, it is still a ghost, even if the dead body has been captured.

(7)

Chris is a thylacine, but he walks on two legs and smokes cigarettes. Because his jaw opens so wide, Chris is good at swallowing things. Because he is a thylacine, Chris is a ghost.

(8)

If Monica and Chris were to capture Monica and Chris and they were both alive or dead and not moving in places apart from their bodies, Monica and Chris would not be ghosts. If Monica and Chris were not ghosts, then Monica could say to Chris "I hereby take you as my lawfully wedded husband" and Chris could say to Monica "I hereby take you as my lawfully wedded wife" and if they were in what are called felicitous circumstances they would thereby be Man and Wife.

(9)

If Monica wandered into my apartment I would call the police so she could be confirmed as Monica. Otherwise Monica would be a ghost and my apartment would be haunted and I would have to move to a different apartment. If Monica wandered into my apartment she almost certainly would be in a fugue state and not dead.

(10)

If Chris wandered into my apartment I would light his cigarette and run my hand along his stripes. I would ask him if he had seen Monica and he would kiss me all over and chafe me with the fur of his snout.

# JACK RABBIT

There was once a boy whose father hunted jack rabbits. The father would shoot them and make them into meals and coats. He would use them well, and the boy knew his father would use them well, but he was still unsure about killing. He would think often of the rabbits, of how they moved and felt, of how they bled. So it was natural, what he did.

He took the golden lamp from his father's shed and rubbed it as necessary, drawing the thin genie from within and thereby procuring the standard three wishes. The boy, being a frugal and sensitive child, decided to use only one wish immediately. He would save the other two for when he had thought of his proper desires.

His first wish was the obvious one. He wished to be a jack rabbit for a day so that he might know the animal's condition. This way he could decide whether or not to hunt them.

And so the boy was transformed into a jack rabbit. He stretched out his new body and spent the morning adjusting to the strangeness of unused muscles, the novel regime of leporid movement, the sweet taste of grass. This body was good and the boy was happy in it.

The afternoon was calm and warm. The sun soaked the boy's fur and lulled him into a forgetful ease in which he wandered within sight of his father's kitchen window. His father, armed as always, spied the jack rabbit and shot him through neatly with a single bullet. He walked outside to gather the body, hung it on a nail in his shed. He'd deal with his catch in the morning, just as soon as he had time.

At the moment though, the father was preoccupied with his son's absence. When the boy did not return overnight, his father telephoned the police to report him missing. Officer Henry was a friend of the family, so he drove to the father's property to help search for the boy.

After a few questions and a cup of coffee, Officer Henry asked the father to show him his shed. It was a good place to start, as children often hide in such dark approximations of houses. The father complied and the two men looked in on the skinning tools and shotguns. There, naturally, lay the boy's body, face down on the floor, bullet-pierced, his weight having dragged him from the nail when his wish wore off.

Officer Henry stared at the boy's father. "Thank God I didn't eat him," said the father. It was a natural reaction. His stomach would have exploded.

# THE HEDGEHOGS ARE GOING TO DINNER

Hedgehogs crowded outside the door, a sea of bristles, stub snouts poking up in the breaks. Inside, a sommelier busied himself inventing flavors to detect. Patrons launched happily into confetes and ceviches, soft items in ramekins. More hedgehogs piled patiently at the entrance. A booted customer crunched blithely across their backs. The maitre d' peered over his mustache. The chefs kept cooking. Table conversation remained lively.

Some miles away, Jim Wadley stretched his fingers at the Saint Sebastian pipe organ. Imitation whale sounds. The local pigeons decamped to a neighboring roof. Another mile west, David and David lay passed out, unseen in the high grass of the median.

More hedgehogs waddled up, a thick-spiked semi-circle working its way around the restaurant. An enterprising waiter tried to shoo them, a sous chef broomed to no avail. Perhaps, thought the maitre d', they would like to be seated?Meanwhile the taller David woke and dug a finger into the dirt. He was sad and a worm wound its way towards his palm. The smaller David stayed deep in dreams. Wadley's organ tones hung softly in the air. The waking David closed his eyes again. The worm continued to climb.

In the lot behind the restaurant, Lynne Abbot sat and skipped rocks. It was easier on concrete than water and she hated difficult things. She had a stack of pebbles on a car hood and sent them bounding into patchy grass at the lot's edge. She too could hear Wadley's organ and tried to time her throws as blunt percussion.

Lynne had seen the hedgehogs gathering across the asphalt, but they'd kept their distance and she felt too dead to muster curiosity. The hedgehogs, for their part, were now largely gone from view, save for a few stragglers who'd showed up too late to be seated. The bulk of them had been ushered in and herded to a series of unoccupied banquet tables at the rear of the restaurant. There the waitstaff carefully lifted the hedgehogs, set them in their chairs, and served a buffet of food scraps that their unexpected clientele devoured.

The Davids, sleeping together now, found that the organ was soundtracking their dreamscapes. They were having a pair of perfectly fitted dreams; the edge of one locking snugly into that of the other. This led to an unstable dreamway along which the pair could freely travel through each other's minds. They walked arm in arm in the smaller David's dream, down a green path in a menagerie, gold cages penning in baboons, mandrills. It was lovely, this perfect match of the unconscious, this chance to tour the psychic world of the other. A David turned and asked: But what if one of us wakes up?

He was right to worry. Lynne Abbot had wandered from the restaurant parking lot. She was angling toward the mountain, not from desire but because of its girth. The grass on which the men slept lay in her path and she was staring at the sky, making up a song to accompany the organ. *Until you come for me/My Worm King/I know I'll long to be/Your warm thing/Oh how I long to see/You each spring/Bright and wriggling/My Worm King/My Worm King.* The song of the Worm King penetrated the Davids' dreamland and their dream selves shuddered. Neither wanted the Worm King to interrupt their idyll.

The Worm King is a single being made of the entwined bodies of thousands of individuals. A myth of course, but a popular one, worms wriggling together, knotted into the shape of a handsome man. He's said to roam the countryside, equally attracting and repelling those who see him. Whenever the Worm King gets close enough to a person, he will embrace them and send his little worms into their ears and nose and mouth and eyes. The person's head will fill and swarm with worms, and they will fall, and the worms will return to the King.

The hedgehogs also have a version of the Worm King legend. For them, he's more like Santa Claus merged with the Gingerbread Man. The Worm King of the hedgehogs comes once a year and feeds his delicious self to the prickly masses. He sacrifices himself, Saint Worm King, irresistible. Should the Worm King come to the little restaurant, the hedgehogs there would be a pack of heroes, but he is only a myth and the hedgehogs are heroic to no one.

In her reverie, still singing, Lynne Abbot stepped on the sleeping head of the smaller David. He jolted awake, screaming. Lynne fled into the dark of the neighborhood. The larger David remained motionless, unresponsive. His voice didn't exactly start speaking in his companion's mind, but what happened was almost like that. Larger David's consciousness lodged there, sharing headspace, able to awkwardly wrest control of motor functions in moments when the body's proper mind relaxed.

In the days that followed, the two Davids would learn to share the body, the smaller David naturally retaining primary control, but ceding it willingly for activities (like chess and baking) at which his companion excelled. They found the arrangement pleasant, actually, and surprisingly convenient. *Two heads may not be better than one*, they would say to each other, silently, at home maybe, or in the Volvo trading shifts on the long drive to the smaller David's mother's condominium, *but two minds certainly are*.

But that unexpected domestic bliss was still to come. On this night they were confused and uneasy as the organ played on, settling fugues into the midnight air. Larger David's body lay dormant, comatose, his head emptied like a Worm King victim. In the restaurant, the hedgehogs finished eating and began to mill in the party room. More were coming. So many more.

Thousands flowed down the mountain, over Lynne who did not flee fast enough, over larger David's body. They packed into restaurants across the city—Denny's and Chez Albert's and the newish Greek place that's supposed to be good. The smaller David hid and watched from the top floor of a parking garage.

The hedgehogs were hungry and they were going out for once. They were so sick of cooking at home. Just one night in a nice place, they were sure, as a species, would really make all the difference.

# PLANTERS

The grayish man stops his walking to stare. One of those objects is in his path. One of those planters.

This one's an arm, hairy, with flowers that grow from its base. Little bluebells bloom where the shoulder belongs. The arm's hand, effete, curls from a limp wrist. The arm is blocking the sidewalk, resting on a diagonal within the concrete square that frames it. Its bluebells grow out and up, describing a curl similar to the hand's but reaching skyward.

The arm is drained of color but is otherwise well-preserved. Its fingernails are too white and the fingertips are just beginning to pucker. The grayish man squats. He would like to enclose the planters in glass. Better, he would shellac them thickly so they'd shine. He does have a camera at least.

A bird plucks a bluebell with its beak. This pleases the grayish man, so he continues walking.

Two days pass.

The grayish man has tacked up twelve pictures of different planters. A dark leg yields wheat, a large hand crawls with honeysuckle. Not far from his house is a clover breast.

At noon, the man begins his normal walk. His scalp itches and feels loamy to the touch. His hair feels thicker, stalkier, dug-in. He passes the same planters in the same places. Today there is a new one, a mossy chunk of thigh beside the Murrow Memorial bench.

A curious thing: the planters have no rot. They seem only to decay so much and then to somehow self-maintain.

The grayish man snaps a picture of the new one. The light's good and there isn't much smog. He pockets his camera and moves on. He fingers and keeps fingering his scalp.

Another day passes.

The grayish man feels constriction in his throat. He pictures his neck withering, his hair growing roots. The strands seem brittle already, hard, as if becoming bark. Still, he continues to walk his circuit, so, as always, he sets out.

His neck feels ever tighter as he walks. He knows this is almost certainly in his head.

The grayish man wouldn't mind if his hairs all became oak trees, or even twined together to become just one, a massive tree, sideways, crowning him.

He sees nothing new on this walk. Thirteen planters sit unmoved and at peace. Once home, the grayish man bathes in the hottest water he can stand. His eyes close.

He's pruned in the morning from an accidental tub sleep. He dries himself and dresses, then begins his walk. It's another clear day. New planters seem always to appear when the weather is so.

This day is no exception. The grayish man stops his walking to stare.

# A ROOM THAT IS AND OR IS NOT PAST TENSE

In the felt room is a softer spot in the soft of the whole. There is a slot there for the cards that poke out each morning and afternoon.

The morning card said Tongue Exercises.

So the morning was for flexing and stretching, for folds.

Afternoon was another easy one, Sitting Still. It was a common card. A favorite.

At night the four people in the felt room slept side by side without touching.

In the morning the card said Diamond Mining and the four people who live in the felt room switched on their helmet lamps and entered the mine shaft. They carted diamonds to the softer spot in the soft whole of the felt room and pressed the diamonds to the slot, which was warm and wet, which one of them swore was pulsed with breath, which one of them swore tasted right. The afternoon card read Handcuff Game and that took the four of them to night.

The slot in the softer spot of the soft of the felt room is not mouth or vagina. The four residents of the felt room are not and are distinct.

The felt room is not heaven or otherwise afterlife. The felt room is not womb or otherwise before life.

The felt room has a relation to life that is best described as non-coinciding.

The four residents slept the night head to foot to head to foot to head to foot to head to foot and not touching at all.

The slot in the morning gave a card that read Waltz and the four residents of the felt room waltzed four hours on the sponged and sinking surface of the felt room floor.

The evening card read Diamond Mining and diamonds were brought in heaps from the deep and glittering shaft.

Night in the felt room has four sleeping bodies non-coinciding.

The felt room does not have coincidence. The felt room is not a photograph but is punctured by a punctum, a slot in the softest spot of its soft self. The felt room can be said to have a self.

Anything can be said of the felt room but that does not make it true. But that does not make it false. But that does not make it false or true. But that does not make it false and or true.

The felt room can be said to have mouth or vagina but the felt room does not have mouth or vagina.

Or the slot of the soft of the soft of the felt room is not mouth or vagina.

The morning card read Vomit and the vomit that the four residents of the felt room vomited they vomited into the slot in the soft of the soft of the felt room because that was not where they slept at night. They vomited in the slot of the soft of the soft because they did not want to vomit in the diamond mine because they used their hands there, roughly, to pry loose those stones.

The afternoon card did not say Escape because no card would say Escape because that would not mean anything in the felt room.

The afternoon card said Sitting Still and smelled faintly of vomit.

At night the four residents of the felt room touched finger to finger to finger to finger.

No.

At night the four residents of the felt room almost touched finger to finger to finger to finger and felt in the small air between finger and finger a pressure or thicker air that was almost skin.

The felt room has a pressure or thicker air that at night is almost skin.

If the air in a room, in any room, would thicken in just the right way and become not just almost skin but skin, then the air in the room would be flesh and no longer fit for breathing.

Then instead of molding each moment to the inside of lungs, the air would instead mold flesh perfectly to flesh, then the air would catch and cast each body enroomed exactly. And if then the bodies in the room in which the air had thickened perfectly to skin were then removed from such a room, then what would be left would be airless cavities that were the exact absences of those gone bodies.

# TODAY FOR JOWLED MARCUS!

Today is a day for Jowled Marcus!

Yesterday for slobbered sitting, another meatball sandwich, one more set of mother's looks. Today is not that day! Today is for Jowled Marcus! To gum back his flaps and crack his knuckles! Today is helmeted and goggled and full of caffeine! Today is the day of the race!

Jowled Marcus circles wide-eyed, flatskinned and fast, great cheeks back-waggling in the absence of a windshield.

They're shooting as ever from the stadium seats. There's a crash and then another! The cars are bursting! The track is piling metal frames. Dr. Morson scuttles wreck to wreck with his leech bucket and ear clippers. His burlap ear bag is nearly full! His leech bucket seems endlessly teeming.

Jowled Marcus keeps to lapping. He is in wind and speed!

Dr. Morson leans and snips at the 22 car. A single motion dispenses an ear and stops the head gape with a sizable leech.

One blood line leaks to the driver's chin, the rest is leeched quite well. Morson hums and strokes the black suckers at bucket bottom. The 12 is still aflame. Morson breaks to let it cool enough for tending.

The grassy center of the oval track is a field of deafened drivers, leech-eared, lurching off-balance towards Jenny Webster. Jenny Webster is passing lemonade. Jenny Webster is passing free lemonade!

Jowled Marcus hugs the rail, drafting tightly in the leader's wake. The stadium shots riddle his helmet. His car stays running and fast, lapping and lapping.

Jowled Marcus is not even thinking once about his mother's pallor, her again, her sandwiches even! Jenny Webster is shining and with lemonade and is the whole total of female space in today completely!

Jenny Webster lives here in the very middle of the stadium and all alone except today. It is today, of the race!

The 19's on rims, tires shot to shreds, barely struggling to the turn. Dr. Morson's gone to gallop, catching up to the limping car and smashing the window with his rock mallet. Jenny Webster's watching, blue-eyed and darling, putting her hands to her face and making that mouth! Dr. Morson reaches in for his cutting, so dextrous, so neat! The 19 spins to the wall, sparking rims a flare to the crowd. Easy target!

Dr. Morson dashes off again, safe and lovely, trailing ears from his overstuffed sack.

The lap-counter shouts 10 to go. Home and forgotten, a Jowled mother is sandwich-cheeked and out of mind. The shooting doubles. Jenny Webster tends the men, wets and sweetens their mouths. Jowled Marcus makes his move amidst the final bullets and grenades. He feints to the outside, cuts back hard as the lead car tries to block.

The cars clash and on comes the crowd fire. Through his left cheek cuts a shot, neatly through, small and hot. Jowled Marcus rams the lead car, eases slightly and fully accelerates. Jowled Marcus is jowl-pierced, speeding, streaming blood back, passing to the front.

Dr. Morson strings his trophies, flowerly, on fishing line. He is smiling and humming, leech-tongued and full of joy.

Today is for Jowled Marcus! Today, of the race, the fastest today! Jowled Marcus slows at last beneath the checkered flag. Jowled Marcus! Today! To the podium and bulletproof glass! To the speech and safe stage! Jowled Marcus is climbing up, flopping and perfect, this pale and victorious boy!

Morson of course gives the oratory. Jowled Marcus bows to the good doctor, baring his neck for the lei of ears. He cups his face and plies his lips, squats and thrusts. Jowled Marcus is preening to capture such applause, such pure love in sound! His mouth he wraps in flaps and muffled-screams his own pure thanks.

Today is this day! For Jowled Marcus! Tomorrow for sulking and mothers and Jenny Webster crying lonely in stadium grass. Today Today Today, Marcus Today, Jowled Marcus Today Forever.

# THE PORK SHUNTER'S FINGERS

1) The Thorough Description of Several Years

She shunted the pork cube along, past her position on the inspection trough. Nothing was green, nothing was crawling. Nothing ever was, so the cubes greased their own way past the shunting women and into packaging.

Her name was Margaret and she worked as the last shunting woman on the quality inspection line, which meant that all the green or crawling things had already been alerted on and redirected well before any product ever reached her. So she passed on the slippery meat, silently, cube by cube with the flat end of a metal prod. Nobody talked much at the plant, and Margaret didn't even do hellos. Proximity had never struck her as a particularly good reason for closeness. Still, nobody disliked her. She came to work, didn't hold up the line, bore a familiarity that was pleasant enough.

Pork shunting was Margaret's job and thus a large part of her identity. Her home life consisted of a sloping and darkening set of untidy rooms, a small collection of known communicants, a boyfriend who went in and out of phase. She persisted in a schedule of shuntings and homeward retreats. Years massed on and around her person just slowly enough that no one was ever alarmed.

2) The Magic That Happened

One day, Margaret realized that her fingers could regenerate. This was during one of her boyfriend's more visible periods. He was at the foldable card table, waiting. Margaret was chopping stewables. She took off her whole index finger with one sure, clean motion.

The things to notice first were the pain and the spreading of blood across her cutting board. Her boyfriend was good to her then. He did the right things in the right order. He found her gauze and medical tape, wrapped the stub and finger separately, and then ushered her to his car. During the drive to the hospital, Margaret's boyfriend spoke mainly about the excellent prognosis for finger reattachment. He was very confident or feigned confidence. He spoke surely as he drove.

In the passenger seat was where she learned that her fingers regenerated. By the time they'd pulled into the hospital parking lot, Margaret had a whole new finger. She flexed it, swirled it in the air. It was perfect and without pain. Her boyfriend turned his car around and headed back to her house. The whole drive he was shaking his head. Margaret took her old, severed finger and threw it out the window to a stray dog. It made them both a little happier.

Next there were weeks of keen experimentation and the improvisation of new routines. Margaret learned the secrets of self-butchery. She calculated the exact speed of her regeneration, how best to staunch her bleeding, the proper dosage of local anesthetics. Tips of fingers and whole digits mounted in her kitchen compost. The garbage swelled with bloodied gauze.

At the pork plant, Margaret began to shave herself into the shunting trough. She'd think to bloody up the meat or sometimes bury a shard of nail or bone. They say that people taste like pigs, maybe a little sweeter. After Margaret, the pork cubes slid into automated packaging. No one would ever notice. Margaret took off a series of knuckles, left them pressed like buttons against the meat.

She was bolder in the bathroom and wrote blood messages across the stalls. She planted thumbs upright in public gardens. Other than that, her life was mostly the same as before. She still didn't say very much, still prodded the safest end of the meat line. It wasn't like anything was actually better.

3) Another Thing Margaret Would Do, and Something She Couldn't

Margaret also had a domestic use for her fingers. With her sharpest blade ready on the bedstand, Margaret and her boyfriend would undress and get into position. She would work a finger up inside of him as far as it would go, cut it off at the base and keep pushing. She'd get it to lodge inside for a few minutes, then it would bleed out and deflate and her boyfriend would shit bones.

While she gauzed up her gaps and applied anesthetic, he'd scrub those little phalanges clean and stack them in the shoebox he kept under the bed. On days Margaret was gone, he would plug himself up with the bones and sit through the afternoon game shows that played on the living room TV.

The last afternoon, she came home to her boyfriend. He was on the faux-leather reclining chair, bone-stuffed and totally still. Margaret laid him out, stomach down, ready. She buried herself in ten fingers deep and they waited for regrowth. This was a new and braver try than ever. Margaret took off her whole arm at the shoulder and bled and bled. It wasn't going to come back.

Her boyfriend picked himself up and tried to do right. What he did was he gauzed her shut and buckled her into the passenger seat of his car. But Margaret just lost too much blood.

Her boyfriend pulled to a stop on the side of the road. His asshole was her mausoleum.

# YOUTH AND BEAUTY

Our neighbors take the bonemeal from the powder of crushed-up bones and mix it with brine and a small amount of lard, then they grind it all into a paste that they spread on their faces and on the faces of their children. Our neighbors and their children wear the bonemeal paste under their eyes the way athletes use paint to deflect the glare of stadium lights.

They have a daughter who is nearly eighteen and very pretty. She likes to watch us when we bathe the dog in the backyard or weed in the vegetable garden. She sits still on a very tall chair that lifts her above the fence between our houses. She tells us things.

"We like the bonemeal paste because it seeps proteins into our skin to keep us youthful and beautiful. Look at my mother. She is stunning."

"What are you doing up on the very tall chair?"

"I'm hoping you'll offer me something to drink. I'm terribly thirsty."

I give her a lemonade. She gives me a wink and produces a thin plastic straw from the breast pocket of her overalls. "This is very good lemonade. Mother and Father never make their own." I can hear her mother and father grinding the bones in the concrete pit behind the fence between our houses

"Where do you get your bones? For the paste I mean, not the bones in your body. I know where those come from."

Our neighbors' daughter sips on her straw and looks at me with both eyes. "Different places. The same places as other bones I suppose." She crosses her legs and continues on the lemonade until the glass is empty and then she calls me over to retrieve it. We both say "Thank you," which may or may not mean anything.

Our neighbors are youthful and beautiful. We hear them driving home in pickup trucks loaded with bones, pulling into their gravel driveway at all hours of the night. I still don't know where they go for the bones. My wife thinks I'm too nosy and should just leave them be. I think she's afraid of what might happen if I find out too much.

Because, you see, we don't know where the bones come from. I don't just mean that we don't know their provenance. We don't even know what kind of animal.

Outside it's too cold for lemonade because it's Christmas. Our neighbors' daughter is standing on our front steps ringing our doorbell. She's holding her finger down on the button and waiting for us to answer. She is holding in her smooth hand a small plastic tub of paste on the exterior of which is neatly hand-lettered "For Faces."

She stares at me without saying anything at first. I take the tub from her hands and lift the lid slightly. The paste is well-mixed and has an even consistency, but I can see the flecks of bone studding it like those exfoliating micro-beads in my apricot facial scrub.

"Merry Christmas."

"Oh, thank you. Merry Christmas to you also."

I smile and close the door. We should have given them something. Now we are indebted. I will have to buy chocolate-covered pretzels and wrap them in cellophane and place them in our neighbors' mailbox.

Upstairs, my wife is calling to me to ask who was at the door. I tell her what happened and she agrees about the pretzels and cellophane. She also tells me to throw away the bonemeal paste. She tells me it's disgusting and we don't know where the bones come from. She's right, so I seal the lid and lay the jar on top of the garbage in our kitchen trashcan.

But when night comes, I can't sleep and the lights are on in our neighbors' house. I can see their silhouettes cast against their window shades. I think I can see our neighbors' daughter dancing. I can see a form moving and I imagine it's her. It's hard to tell what's happening exactly. My wife is sleeping soundly in her usual nightgown. I think about waking her and pointing out the figures in the window, but instead I go to the trashcan and take out the little tub marked "For Faces."

I take off the lid and can smell the paste. It smells strong, like a slow-cooking pot of stew. I scoop out a large glob with my index and middle fingers and leave the tub on the tiled island in our kitchen. Of course the thing to do next is to go back upstairs and tuck myself into bed and gently massage the bonemeal paste into the skin of my wife's sleeping face.

# BRIGHT PAPER/BLOOD SAND

In the time of the end times, the world is in shambles. Things have nowhere to go but up.

So the survivors make a pyramid of ruined people—flimsy, often limbless bodies, piled one on top of the next, up and up towards the moon.

A pair of plastic surgeons figure to cash in on this ruin, on so many broken mouths and breasts and body-things. The surgeons build a bright new office in anticipation, but because all of them are ruined, the people decide they don't need to be fixed. And so the plastic surgeons, ruined themselves, get no new patients. They sit and glumly sharpen-shine their knives.

The surgeons cut their wallpaper into long strips and wrap up the statues in the park. Then they cut up the wallpaper in other offices and use it to wrap still more.

They're preparing the statues as gifts.

All the while, people keep crawling up the human pyramid, getting higher and higher in the thin air and eating the curious birds they catch with their teeth.

There are sports fields in the pyramid's shadow. Ruined bankers have taken up volleyball. They push their skins to the net mesh for the feel of it. White sand cakes their ragged feet. The volleyball court is a bloodslick ringed with depressed spectators.

There's someone keeping score by scoring his arms with a knife, one cut per point and a hash mark every fifth. It's hard to tell who is winning.

Towering over the wrapped statues and blood sand, the human pyramid people all stick out their tongues as it rains. They rise, a mile-high block of broken bodies and extended tongues, crushing one another and trying to drink from the air.

The surgeons, out of statues, drag their bags to the pyramid base. They've got miles of vinyl between them. They've got spackle and tape too. The bottom bodies are mostly dead, having days ago eaten all the grass and bugs in face range. One surgeon opens a dead mouth and uses the teeth as a clamp to fix the first wallpaper strip. He and his partner begin the long loop around the pyramid. Once around the base, they paper higher.

They circle ever upwards, entombing, a little proud as they paste over face after face.

From a distance, the individual pyramid people appear indistinct. Instead one sees colors: pastel yellow, teal and violet, the dun of human scaffolding. The surgeons perch at the end of their work. Bright paper rises over blood sand.

# MOTHER TONGUE

We're speaking of your tongue, how it regenerates, how you cut it over and over from your mouth, how the blood pools in the cave of your lower lip until you spit it out and parcel us your tongue in strips. You use your front teeth then, them a sieve to strain the blood, to shift its path to ground. For the time after, you like to sit listening, sometimes humming, while we partake and take to speaking of your tongue.

For speaking of your tongue of course we use the other tongue of yours, your language, that called tongue not eaten.

Tongue growth takes an hour and then, again, you can scalpel us mouth muscle, lay it on the skillet, season neatly with lichen and onion grass. I collect the water from the rock trickle and the twins set to scavenging what growths can be gathered. I collect also your spat blood in the blood pail for boiling to broth.

We're speaking around the constant fire that when you spoke you called 'eternal flame.' We lit it from the dregs of the last of the gasoline pumps. This was when there was still canned food and you would call the daylight 'school time' and cage the twins in the metal shopping cart. School time was when you pointed and spoke and with your fingers helped me right my mouth. Later, the twins came also to speech and I was called Teaching Assistant or TA or my last little TA and it was good that those days you kept my hair a length for tousling.

I'm telling you this because you ought to hear how I remember the time between the times your body fed me. I know that then was when you felt most mothersome and tenderhearted. You should know I know you past your meat.

But you see Mother, the twins, the twins who came late to speech and never into proper names, the twins have cast their votes together as always. And Mother, I fear you ought not to have passed on democracy as part of our inheritance.

After the first growth or miracle, when your tongue returned (though we all saw it flat on the floor, severed from your seizure biting), you said, 'You see, your mother is indeed a saint!' And on the second accidental bite-through, you again were so happy to feel it re-grow. 'God knows,' you said, 'I've still some things to teach!'

But you must admit that your tongues have taught less and less since the food stock ran out. We agreed then that the places for tongues are mouths, and we agreed also that slicing was worth an attempt, and then it returned and you spoke of your 'prodigal tongue.' We cheered then, all of us, remember? The twins and I gave praise in hunger as you braised your tongue on the fire.

It was one tongue daily for each of us for some time after, until our growing required more cuts to sustain us. Now you only reserve a working tongue for the lecture hour. Do you not see your progression to silence? This change is really only a continuation.

We took the vote while you were sleeping. And as the twins are two and I am only one, well, who was I to vote at all? Your own vote, beside my held-tongue, could not have saved yours, so I felt no compunction to wake you, chose instead to let you sleep in peace.

But now is no longer time for words.

Now is time to open wide.

# MALDOROR, SUFFERING FROM KIDNEY FAILURE, TAPES HIS WEEKLY TELEVISION PROGRAM

*A camera films a face that looks straight-on. The room is beige and the camera does not move. The face starts to speak:*

Hello and Hello! This week we'll begin with some premises, a few facts about myself:

My body is coated in hard sharp hair. I have a hooked barb instead of a penis. My face is a sandpaper desert. No matter where, you must bleed to caress me.

I'm sorry. I don't know why I say the things I say when I'm on TV. Let me start over: This is a situation comedy. The situation is that I'm dying.

I used to think *dialysis* was *dial a sis*. I thought it was some kind of cross-dressing sex hotline, not a washing machine for blood.

I will break this machine and wash this whole office with blood. I will stain this carpet to have left some kind of mark somewhere, some big fading illegible blot.I probably will not do any of the things I say when I am on TV.

We will open your mouth with a crowbar and turn it into our hiding cave. I'm the star of this program but I'm sick of you people seeing me. We will live in your molars, I mean it.

When I say 'we' I mean me and the other characters on this television program.

When I am on TV like now I say whatever I want to say because the TV will make it true. That man with the barbed-hook penis lives in the cameraman's mouth, someone will say. I heard it on TV they will say.

I really will build a fortress of lost and broken-off teeth. I promise I will, using carpenter's glue. Please send me your toothsome envelopes. I live at 275 North Street in Buffalo, New York. We will build it together if you want to come over.

I might tear out your kidneys and try to tape them into my side or glue them into my side with carpenter's glue.

Whenever I am on TV is when I talk this way. I promise this is true, like everything I say on TV.

I am the main character in this situation comedy. The other characters are a chair with eyes and a squid that looks more like a jellyfish. The other characters I drew with my own one hand.

I will draw characters on the outside of your kidneys if I get my hands on them.

I will mark up your kidneys so bad that your blood will need a good long cleaning.

We can watch old video tapes of Richard Pryor because after all this is a comedy.

I will draw the other characters in this TV show all over the front of your camera and pull out your teeth and kidneys and build things out of them and draw all over them.

I will pull the pieces out of you and leave myself all over them.

We can laugh at the comedy videos on the television screen.

My face is for the camera a beautiful scrap of sandpaper to make love to. This is a situation comedy. Next week: my spurting catheter malfunction that will ricochet, if you send yours, off my wall of donated teeth.

So again, your teeth. Send them to me please and may they fall out in droves for my using.

And until this time next week, endless night, rotten luck!

# DEAD KIDS

We aren't going to do so well, I am thinking, even though I used to be in the top quartile easy. Here they give us the worst teachers because they know we aren't going to take so many State Assessments. Dad says it makes sense because how else is this country ever going to compete with the Chinese if all our best teachers are teaching dead kids? And since the union won't let them get fired, who else should the bad teachers teach?

Mom says not to call us dead kids and Dad says I know what he means.

Mr. Baker is the worst teacher they can't fire. He's in charge of Social Studies and History, which are actually the same thing. We are learning about the Civil War or Rights Movement. Mr. Baker says that when things in history are called *Civil*, they are usually about helping Black people. I am vomiting into a bag and shuddering, sloshing the nutrient water in my IV. Martin Luther King was neither Martin Luther nor a King. Virginia was against Loving but for Lovers, at least on their shirts. My aide is taking notes because it's hard for me to write while I am vomiting so much, so prone to torn skin, to spontaneous bleeding. Halloween this year Dad shaved his head and called himself Yul Brynner after Mom said he couldn't tell people he was going as me.

My aide is Robert Butler and he is taller than me and played high school beach volleyball. I told him I was old enough that I wanted to touch a penis once and please and now he doesn't sit so close that I can smell him. I wanted to try it out in my mouth but he's afraid I'll vomit on it, which is a reasonable thing to be afraid of.

Today especially, I would vomit all over it, even if it was the best mouth-fit ever. Right in the middle of English I am shaking so hard and vomiting spray. English is Mrs. Fritz. Whenever she says Charles Dickens all us dead kids giggle and Robert Butler writes down Charles Dickens in my notes. Today Robert Butler is wheeling me out to the hall and the nurses because you can't projectile vomit and stay in class.

The nurses take me to my own room. They lay me out and measure me many ways and I don't stop convulsing. Dad is there, awkward-looking in his new hair, and in a slightly better moment he asks how I'm doing. Mom is not looking. I say we have testing next week and Dad is thinking good thing they gave me Mr. Baker but all he says is maybe you shouldn't worry so much about that.

# FAMILY VACATION FACTS

The small perfect French child had on a bright blue fire truck sweater. Underneath the sweater he wore a collared dress shirt and below the sweater he wore tight jeans and fresh red Converse sneakers. The small perfect French child was flying with his father, presumably back to France, though possibly to Quebec or certain parts of Belgium or Switzerland. It's hard to tell accents when you don't really know the language.

The small perfect French child did not have a mother. Because she was not with him, she did not exist. His father must have crafted him out of supplies like flesh and glue. This is naturally why the child was so perfect and so small. This is naturally why his aesthetic was impeccable.

The father was less perfect than his son. The father must have had a mother and father of his own. Fathers don't need mothers and fathers present in order to have them. Fathers stand on their own and often are slightly past due for a haircut.

The small perfect French child applied exactly the proper amount of pressure to his father's fingers. He was good at things like holding hands. Being perfect, he was good at most things.

The father and his child did not realize it but the woman behind the desk was not really an airline attendant. She was an airline attendant, but not only. Not mainly. The woman was a spy. She was really a spy!

# CHILDPAINTER

Arnold was the childpainter. He could do other things—furniture, sunsets—but ultimately he was the childpainter. Sometimes you just are what you are.

Now, childpainter meant a few things. First it was only portraiture. Just as some people make whole careers painting thoroughbred horses or pet memorials, Arnold was sought out only for his paintings of youths. He had a way of pulling out the perfection of children that faded in his pictures of teenagers and was gone entirely for any subjects beyond their early twenties. The adult portraits didn't lack for competence, but they lacked for something else, something more important and less easy to define.

In his early years, Arnold fancied himself a landscape painter. He loved hills and dunes, any kind of mound. He loved things rounded off and worn out, things in slow decay. Even early on, Arnold preferred not to be overwhelmed.

How he came to childpainting was through a commission. A family friend in need of portraiture approached Arnold with a modest (but to Arnold generous) offer and Arnold, still a student at the time, completed the painting while on summer break from Cranbrook. Onerecommendation led to another and soon Arnold was painting the children of the upper crust through a whole swath of the Mid-Atlantic. He was not unhappy in this work and in little time he had abandoned his precious landscapes in favor of the lucrative business of rendering wealthy children as they ought to be.

By his thirties, Arnold had moved beyond simple representation. He began to paint on the children directly, right along with their portraits, so that the real children did not seem unworthy imitations of their images.

That was what had been happening. The children were beginning to disappoint. Parent after parent called Arnold to say that they loved the portrait but now had noticed something off about their child, a lack of spark, some new ungainliness.

Arnold realized that childpainting could not go only in one direction. He had first to paint the picture of the child in order to capture a perfect image-version. Then he must go on to transpose the perfection of the portrait onto the actual child. Upon completion of a work, Arnold could then send the child out, portrait in hand, beauty matching beauty, twin poles of an aesthetic whole.

The parents, of course, loved such retouched progeny, at least at first. The children were radiant until the paint wore off or (once Arnold addressed that problem with more resilient paint) stretched apart into patches across the growing skin of their young bodies. That is, in time the children became a series of blotched and ruined paint jobs. The parents would send their children back to Arnold for revision, but he could only do so much for them as they aged out of his range. Each new painted child became the scene of inevitable dissatisfaction, of the future uncanny, of the visible deterioration of youth into young adulthood.

When his clientele realized what lay in store, Arnold's commissions began to dry up. He had become accustomed to a level of financial success, and so, to supplement his income, Arnold tried painting their lost childhoods back onto adults. The results were unsettling, borderline garish. His subjects could barely stand to look at themselves and Arnold, on the brink of despair, very nearly gave up painting altogether.

It was during this lowest period of his professional life that Arnold hit upon the final iteration of his practice. He thus began a series of death portraits, sitting with the bodies of children, painting them, fixing up their faces for the funerals. He worked quickly, painting only in the time between the embalming and the viewing, often working through the night, molding and painting the faces of the children, perfecting each to a high angelic beauty.

Once a child was finished, Arnold would pull out his easel and his canvasses and hurry to capture his subject's now-permanent grace. This was the most difficult part, as Arnold would, by this point, be exhausted. Still, he always painted two identical portraits of each child. The first he painted for free, a gift for the grieving family. The second portraits were sold to collectors. They are considered highly desirable.

# OCTOPUS

M., lover of octopus, sold tinsel craft in the barge yard. Next door, meanwhile, a warehouse of gelatin lingered on the brink of overheating.

We benched ourselves across from the craft stall where M. wound metal into sparkling ships. Her shirt pattern linked octopi—tentacles coming to nodal points in the weave of their images. Five years ago she'd been a department store salesgirl in a faded corner of the Midwest. Her father owned a house there, from where the fine men had absconded with her brother.

We'd lived like lives in equally unlikely settings and, like M., our brothers had been taken early from us.

M. penciled tentacles in the margins of a discarded receipt. We waited patiently and at ease in the knowledge that she would not recognize us before the boat came. It had been years and we were really only ordinary.

There were four of us and one of M. and five coming brothers. And let's not forget the heat, the impending gelatin melt that at some point passed over to presence in the form of a slow and viscous wave, not unlike the famed Boston molasses surge, low though, and spreading out in colorful liquefaction. Our five brothers were due to arrive at evening. It was fitting for men of their stature, not one shorter than seven foot nine.

—

Real ships lowing. Tinsel replicas strung up and bobbing in the wind.

Gel creep under the door gap, pooling and settling around our shins. M., slightly elevated, oblivious.

—

M. will leave this story in a larger boat, a faded luxury liner. That Bobby Darin song, *Beyond the Sea*, filling in her absence.

—

Our brothers though. They were why we'd come, and they'd come for M., so she too was why we gathered here.

Our brothers, you will have by now guessed, were those disappearing giants about whom the papers had once spilled so much ink. You remember that night when our dozen tallest teens inexplicably vanished? The tales that filtered out later of strange men snooping through our towns in fancy dress? All our young giants had been kidnapped and we, their average siblings, had been too small for their abductors' attentions.

Then there was nothing but rumor for ages and our giants were largely forgotten.

Now, finally, we would learn what had happened.

We'd been given word that the living brothers, ours and M.'s, had been released. We couldn't wait—they were coming here to meet us. M. had not been alerted; she was meant to be surprised.

The seven others were gone. They had disappeared twenty years earlier and it's well-known that giants die young.

We watched M. hum softly as evening came. The gelatin hardened to a smooth new floor. It was festively bright and sticky and represented nothing but the glossed accidental beauty of industrial disaster. M. was patient, as were we, and the giants' ship pulled finally into port.

Our massive brothers wading through reconstituted gelatin, embracing us. M. watched and could recall it all so touchingly later. Her own brother, Gregor, handed her a live octopus in a water-filled glass cube. It had a handle on it like a briefcase. She'd cried in waves of shock and happiness, held her octopus, her brother.

—

Giants are known to die young, remember. The heart has trouble with such bodies.

—

The tallest man in history died of an infection that he failed to notice; his poor circulation made it so he could not feel his feet. He was only twenty-two.

—

M. stared at her new octopus, pressed her face to the case glass. Her brother's heart was giving out. The other giants stood around him in a half-circle. They leaned heavy on their canes. Gregor gripped his sister's shoulders. He had something to say. He could barely keep on his feet.

Our brothers were not the invincible titans we'd built up in our minds. They were the inelegantly slumped armatures for a variety of braces—leg, back—and worse than ill-fitting clothes.

Gregor had come home to die. He leaned over and told M. in the huddle of giants. Our brothers had been his de facto hospice aides, but now M. will take over those duties. Come morning she'll pack her tinsel boats and new octopus and dying brother onto a cruise ship. She'll push him along on a wheeled hospital bed and wait out the end en route to the childhood home in which her brother wants to be buried.

—

Tomorrow M. will be gone. For now we leave her and wander with brothers of our own. We each take the hand of the giant we'd come for and walk from the market to the dock.

We look up at our brothers and are unsure what to ask. They are too thin and want to hear about our lives, our parents. We stand in the clear air of the boardwalk and fill them in on all the banalities they've missed. Our brothers loom and stagger and smile in ways we can't interpret.

It is night and we have endless questions.

Our brothers tell us that they will die soon too, that we shouldn't talk of their missing days, but can we just walk slowly with them now? So we do, the eight of us, along the water, into the dark.

# THE GIRL WHO COULD NOT DROWN

It's new, that squid painted on the ceiling, dripping itself onto her bedspread, onto the small visible part of her hair. She's asleep now, alone, with knives in each hand. When they were a they, the knives stayed underneath their pillows.

When they were a they was almost a long time ago. One thing she can remember is the sex, but not all of it. That afternoon, in a fit of busyness, she'd taped up the squid stencil and laid plastic sheeting on the bed below. She'd spread the paint on thick with a roller brush, left it to dry,

She'd watched TV, made some food. She thought the ceiling was dry, so went to bed thinking she could lie safe beneath. As the girl slept, her squid dripped his ink all over her bedroom and the ceiling caved in and became the ocean.

Her squid gained his third dimension and she woke to the feeling of drowning. When they were a they, this never would have happened. They'd have been too busy with each other for painting the ceiling. Even if this had happened, they'd've swum to the surface with ease, with pure and strong strokes, and together, and smiling.

Her lungs filled with water and the squid inked her, circled her bluing body. His oval eyes watched her sink with her bed. He wrapped her in his tentacles and shot his way surfaceward. The girl wanted only her bed, her pillows. She wanted only the sinking sensation of sinking. She slashed out with her knives, into the tentacles that bore her up into the air. She gasped for breath, sliced down, cut open the squid so he bled a stain on her body.

The squid, wanting but unable to cry, released her into the waves. He felt the salt water clean his wounds. He loosed a jet of ink and headed down to deeper water.

The girl licked squid off her knives.

Alone with the waves, the girl laid herself face-down, letting her hair halo around her. A gull took interest in a strand as it floated in the water. Other gulls arrived, beaked her hair, flew forward to lift her head into breathing.

More gulls came, dug into the skin of her legs and back, lifted those parts of her too. Only her hands hung to the water. Her knives cut the ocean in two parallel lines.

The gulls dropped the girl on an island's beach, in warm black sand, on which she went back to sleep. Her squid swam near the beach to be close. The gulls walked about, pecked after crabs. They smashed the crabs against rocks to puncture the shells and then sucked out the raw flesh inside.

If the girl woke, she was surrounded by crab shells and sitting gulls. She would cut the shells to strips with her knives and tile a section of beach. The fruit here would be plentiful. The squid would wave his healing tentacles from the water. And it would always be warm here, and bright.

# YOU ARE TODAY A MAN

Today Simon, by this archaic measure, you have become a man. Do you believe it? Does anyone in the room? Regardless, we both, you and I, we both have a speech to deliver.

And as it is tradition, I thought at first to make this speech in the standard form of pride and praise. I wrote that speech. I did. I wrote that speech and Rabbi Zucker approved and even lauded it, and I will admit it had a certain beauty, a certain perfection, a pathos found in the fabric of its loving fiction.

It was easy enough to begin with a truth, the typical telling of a flaw in your person, a cause for worry designed to draw laughs. But then came the hard lie of gentling out my insults, the always-lie of telling my surprise at the remarkable person you've become.

Though yes, in a manner of speaking, you are worthy of remark. The obvious place to start being either your head or your birth, both overly watery, stretched too long, smeared in blood. Neither being a bit beautiful or having even the whiff of miracle about them.

To be fair, I've never seen a beautiful baby and only rarely does a head augur more than dim cruelties. And no, you have not been an unmitigated disaster. I do remember a moment I felt tenderness; an image of you that was at least striking, at least worth recalling. This was after you smashed your face against Denny Johnson, for once a time of swelling instead of blood. Your mother had nothing frozen but a rack of ribs that she pressed to your eye so as to swallow your face in thawing meat. Remember how you lay there moaning? How you dripped freezer melt on that t-shirt we bought you when you were on that soccer team for which you never started?

Even now I imagine you rib-faced, the meat and bones to screen and muffle those hacks from your throat that pass for language. To think at thirteen you still so awkwardly shape your tongue to your teeth. Today, as I was to feel such pride, I could only cringe and hide my shame in deep davening. Imagine me, looking out amazed at these people with their regretted checks already made out in your name. Here I was, bowed over, prayerful, thinking how in good faith could I deliver such a lying speech? How could I read those cards that would sound sour and false to any person with an even passing knowledge of your character? And so this rough and off-the-cuff performance will have to suffice as my contribution to your coming of age. Here then, my hopes, your speech:

Son, we see today that you've survived to thirteen, that you've even memorized a rough recital of these Hebrew noises. This is what must count as accomplishment. There's little else; besides that rib-faced spell, I can recall nothing about your youth that one could reasonably celebrate.

However, my Simon, I am not yet ready to give up on you entirely. From this stubborn place of paternal optimism, I can now salvage something of the usual ritual—that traditional father-speech moment in which the elder Jew imparts upon his child a bit of tailored advice.

What I suggest is to daily wake and bind your face in frozen meat. Thereby that oblong head and dull face you carry will be transformed into a site of mystery and feeding dogs. What I imagine for you is blindness set upon by leaping hungry beasts, your body pawed to the ground, your ribbed mask torn to bits morningly, until your skin is open to the teeth and tongues of dogs each day and each day after.

# EXERCISES

EXERCISE #1—JOURNALING

This page you are reading should also be printed in braille. The opposite page should be this page but in braille and might even be if this is printed how it ought to be.

The braille should be knobbed and hard and black. If I have been allowed, if I have been given such grace and budget, the braille is thick-smeared with nutrient paint. It is apricot braille and tea tree oil.

If this is printed in braille and nutrient-smeared on the page opposite this page, you should take the page opposite this page and press it hard to your face. Scrub and press with this text of cleansing abrasion. Raw your face with this text if this text is proper and braille.

Raw yourself to a thin, clean, fresh-skinned face. Let the page opposite this page that is printed with this text as braille text become the well of your oils and the teeth to scuff away your dying.

This page should be a new page. This page should be the next page after the page that has been printed in braille and after the back of the page that has been printed in braille because the back of the page that has been printed in braille should have been and possibly was left blank as a canvas for the seeping through of your skin and dirt and oils. The back of the page that is or should have been printed in braille is or should have been a Rorschach test or oracle in which to read your cleanliness or fate. The darkened, wetted paper that is your excess that is what the back of the page that is or should have been printed in braille is or ought to be is or ought to be called autobiography.

EXERCISE #2—WRITING WHAT'S RIGHT FOR THE MOMENT

Did you shower and drink beer in the shower? Did you set the water to the hottest that you can take and then push yourself to improve yourself at your extremes by then increasing the temperature by one degree?

If you have pushed yourself to improve yourself at your extremes by increasing the water temperature to one degree beyond what you can tolerate and you did not drink any beer in the shower, drink six beers.

If you did not desire a better self through wet heat and you did not drink any beer in the shower, you are not in an appropriate state of being and should not complete EXERCISE #2 until tomorrow.

If you drank beer in the shower, telephone the first person of the same sex that you secretly desired but never admitted desire to and tell that person that you wished always a little or more than a little for them to take you up in a secret and out-of-time space and roughly do with you what you only ever at that time had done with yourself.

Transcribe.


EXERCISE #3—WRITING WITH CONSTRAINTS

Take every sixth word in this exercise and pretend that you love someone you ought to but can't quite. Take someone like your last significant other.


EXERCISE #4—WRITING WHAT YOU KNOW

Cut your face shaving. Cut your legs shaving. Mix the leg blood and face blood in the water of your stopped-up sink. Take a sheet of the most expensive paper you can afford and dye it in the blood sink.

Hang this expensive blood paper to dry. Do not use a hair dryer, towel, fan, or other device. This sheet of paper should dry by hanging in the air, dripping and staining slowly into what will be its proper final mottling.

Write the name of the person you most love in the world and write that name over that name and write that name over that name and write that name over that name again and again on the expensive piece of blood-stained/blood-mottled paper until you cannot even read that name, until the name of the person you love most in the world has blackened and blotted and massed onto itself so thoroughly as to tear entirely through your thick, expensive self-bloodied sheet of paper, until that name has indelibly impressed itself in the oak of your desk.

EXERCISE #5—WRITING FROM PROMPTS

Burn every photograph of your family that you own and imagine that they have disowned you. Describe your memories of the photographs you have just burned and then insert the phrase 'who molested me' after every mention of a family member.

Send this text to your mother and father for Christmas and transcribe their responses when you talk to them about it on the telephone. Replace all uses of the word 'love' with the phrase 'lust after' and replace all mentions of sadness with historical asides about famous shipwrecks.

Send this text to your mother and father along with a series of photographs of your bruised and naked body. Title the photograph series *Arousal*. Videotape your mother and father weeping in response and write a short text describing their physical failings in such moments of discomposure. Write as if your mother and father are naked, writhing, dripping with sweat.

Remember that 'creative writing' means 'the shameful exploitation of everyone who you have ever loved or been loved by in exchange for marginal personal gain.'

# ME, I'M LOOKING OUT

The fur-green of the hills is trees. Dendro- or Derma-, there's not so much difference. Either way's a coating; either way's a shag of stalks. Right now I'm on a bus and bound towards a girl in the northwest of the northeast. What that means is that this is a hopeful writing, a prose of promise. A pro(mi)se. The *mi*'s encapsulated, a note in the middle, as on a scale, and also a homophone for the subject. Me, I'm bussing. Me, I've got a job for the first time in months. So me, I'm busy. You've no reason to care. So.

To make this a story for you, here is a twist or plot event: Swarm of insects, a black cloud engulfing this bus I'm on. What will happen is the cloud will grow and thicken. The air will gum with wings. The cloud will become blanket, atmosphere, and the bugs will lift this bus right off the road. It will be an airbound bus and I'll be dead in the center of a dead black floating.

The bus will touch down in the center of a forest in north-central Pennsylvania where the woods are thick with trees and churches. Often churches are topped with nipple-shaped steeples. Often steeples are called phallic too. This is why God is in all of us, man and woman. Even through clear windows, it's easy to see things wrong. Yesterday my roommate saw a dog's penis and thought it was a breast. The hills look haired. My eyes are tricked by un-bare moundings. Foliage for follicles or reversed, it's all a problem of optics.

A problem of optics——this time a lack of light. Though we'd have lit upon the ground, the insect swarm still will blacken our windows. I will see nothing, no women, no trees, no fur. I will grow from fearful to angry to mostly only sad.

*Dear Insects*, I will trace with my finger in the mass of their bodies—they will have made it into the bus by now and begun to fill up the pockets of air. *Dear Insects*, I will trace. *Dear Insects, I am trying to get to a girl and it's important. I am happier with her, you see. Much. Why did you steal this bus? Why have you dropped me in this particular wood? Please take me instead to her town. Please let me exit there with her.*

And—and this depends on your cast of mind as much as my own, as remember for whom this whole narrative digression was made in the first place—perhaps then the swarm of insects would feel my finger on their many bodies and would lift up the bus once again. And they would fly swiftly to a town, maybe even the right one.

# CAN YOU CALL A GHOST YOUR GIRLFRIEND IF SHE WON'T SAY YES?

Ghosts live under the front porch in the rusted old bucket next to the faucet. They come out of the faucet when you run it to water the grass and they pile themselves into the bucket where the other ghosts give them towels to dry off.

These are slender ghosts. They are pale and lean and come out covered in water. They live together all piled in the bucket and make rooms for themselves in the flakes of rust on the bucket's insides. At night I can hear them singing old ghost songs to each other in perfect alto voices. There are mostly altos, with a few sopranos and mezzo sopranos as well. The ghosts sing songs with titles like 'When I Get To Heaven' and 'Lord, Let Me Be At Peace'.

One of the ghosts is in love with me. I am not sure if this ghost is a boy ghost or a girl ghost or even if ghosts understand gender the same way we do. I prefer to think of this ghost as a girl, because she sings in a high and beautiful voice and curls around my ear while I am asleep. She doesn't answer my questions and I sometimes wonder if she hears me or even can hear me. Her singing seems unrelated to the things I tell and ask her.

She sings about how much she loves me and the ways in which I brush my teeth and hair. I ask her what she did before ghosting and what her name is and all the sorts of getting-to-know-you questions one might ask a lover. I ask her about the people and ghosts she's dated in the past and she sings about the Civil War.

I guess maybe she is from the Civil War, but it's hard to tell. Sometimes she leaves my side and floats in front of me and gives me a little wave with her translucent hand and flies off to the rusted bucket beneath the porch. I think she lives in the bottom, in a deep rust crater where the dirt has started to push through and mix in with the metal. She gathers with the other ghosts and welcomes the new arrivals when they come out of the faucet. In her hands is a little piece of rag that she rubs over the lithe, new, dripping-wet ghosts until they are shining and dry and I am so so jealous.

# MRS. VAN PELT'S CLASS IS NOT COMING TO THE ASSEMBLY

Allison's all covered already in those black and purple welts that make you fear her father. That girl's got the reasons so nobody bothered to ask why. The how is she buried herself alive and left a note we didn't need to read.

Willie got told his mouth was too big for his head one too many times, so he just opened himself up. He ratcheted that jaw right open & mawing wide. He wrapped his upper lip right over the back of his little head and kept going, kept pulling back his front teeth 'til they came up square against his bottom ones. What a clattering! What a clattering they made! Those teeth of his racketing on and on like a sewing circle.

Melissa's mother fed her piecemeal to the wolves until she was nothing left but a concept. Well, a concept hasn't got much in the way of meat, so those hungry wolves ate her mother too.

Darryl had his bones removed one by one and replaced with electric eels. Boy could Darryl dance then! 'Til them eels stung him to death, then he flopped around the floor like a third-rate break dancer. Then them eels died too.

All those other children are only xeroxes, cut out real careful from their cardstock and pasted up in their chairs. Mrs. VP, she does their homework every night in 20 different handwritings. Well, so none of them have to get held back. But come on, they're not about to walk to any auditorium! And Mrs. Van Pelt, her arms would just get tired out carrying them.

# THE FUTURE OF DOGFIGHTING IN AMERICA

These humane days they're teeth-pulled and declawed, pawing and gumming 'til the loser walks off bored and mouth-slimed. Cruel's a sport where our dogs tear out throats and bleed dead for the crowd. Now we garter belt them, slip in dollar bills for the slinkiest. Watch them dogs shake and slobber. They smile and wag, bruise each other up with blunt force.

I rub mine down with no-stick PAM, work that fur gleaming and greased so no jaws can clamp his body. Just last week he took three hundred in slipped tips, cantering round the dirt pit, all mean and slippery. My boy's pure Rottweiler and dark-coated. I've seen him gum a pit bull round his neck and lift that animal airborne so fast that other dog screamed womanly and shit liquid streams right into the crowd. My boy, they called him winner right there and banned that shitting pit for life.

Those clean-shirted boys and all, they don't want to see bloodsport. So we listened. We took out the blood part, made the whole a slower greased-up spectacle, made it all the more like exotic dance. I stuff a five into my Rottweiler's belt and he sees fit to turn things back to nasty. He knows bred into him, a fight's for killing. So he sidles down onto that Doberman, greenbacks rippling fringe in his garter, and he traps that other snout between his buttered chest and the packed dirt. And he waits, and we all wait, and the Doberman's not kicking beneath my boy's weight and the noise of the crowd.

# STORY OF EYES

A car drive on a poorly lit road, fireflies, two glass eyes rolling loose in the passenger-side cup holder. She takes them in her hand, presses them too closely together. Glass-friction soundtracks the way home, all those hours of distance, borders, of changing light and continuous land.

An automatic-opening garage door, a cool bed, a too-soon morning. Three cups of coffee. Too much cream, a failing attempt at two thousand calories per day.

She is named Ellie, describes herself as early-mid-career, a sort of ordinal life point.

She has a dead man's eyeballs in her purse. The glass ones are in her purse. The real ones, the nerve-stringed, blooded, bodily eyeballs, they're in solution, in their own glass with its own light bulb. Ellie keeps those at home.

A glass eye as lozenge. She can think of other things; she's read Bataille.

Glass eyes in photographs, glass eyes close-mic'd, recorded. Reams of magnetic tape sped and slowed. His grinding eyes, that awful drone. Her grinding eyes. The glass pupils are a bolder blue than the organics. Maybe it's just that they've faded, memories and photographs too. Maybe he called the eye sculptor and asked for the sharpest blue in stock. Ellie's tongue slides his eye along the back of her teeth, lips open to the microphone. Glass on enamel, a rhythm based on teeth width of her teeth.

Work time. She dries the eye, folds it in silk, sinks it to the bottom of her purse. An automatic-opening garage door, a silent drive. Her name tag pinned through the weave of her shirt. Eight smiling hours of fixed returns, stipulations, new accounts. It's better than telling.

Pattern and routine, mounting of tapes. Ellie notices the visible aging of her skin, tries creaming it back in time, feels only moistened and odored. She's lit their case and is staring right into those blue and desiccating eyes. Formaldehyde can only do so much. Glass though, glass is forever.

They met when he was old but not yet blind or dying. Ellie liked that she was too young for him. She pretended then that experience counted for something, that a man could age attractively. She liked that he held her hand gingerly.

He was the kind of William who never abbreviated his name, tucked in his shirts, purchased aperitifs. A tall William, past-handsome and easily summed up, not yet aware that his eyeballs had become microbial habitat. They had a good lunch and charmed each other.

There was dating, emotional intimacy, soft, tentative, vaguely unsettling sex. A month or so passed, enough time to establish the image of idyll. The truth of the early weeks is that they were just good enough to bear later exaggeration.

She remembers when William got the stinging in his eyes. It was nothing, scattered dull pricks. Then more pricks that were points of pain, throbbing constellations that intensified for days. Ellie became the bearer of ice packs, ibuprofen, TV trays of simple foods she'd fork into his mouth while William tried to retreat behind his eyelids. Their conversation fell to 'open-your-mouth's and non-linguistic grunts, barely-signifying expressions of air.

The pricks became bars of pain, crosshatched ocular burnings. William would have writhed if he could have beared to move. Ellie called a neighbor and loaded William into her car. There were days of hospital lights, practiced bedside manner, so much sea foam green. Nothing could stop the degeneration of his eyes. They were already only a network of tunnels, eaten out by microscopic mouths.

So the eyes went. William liked to say he clawed them out himself, calmly and neatly, hardly even bleeding. Of course he had them removed by a surgeon, had them professionally stored. He let her walk him out by his hand, drive him and lead him back to his now-strange house.

Ellie recalls it all as lists. Events and sense memories strung together with invented causal relations:

*At first I had felt chained, like this man was in such pain, so helpless, that who was I to leave him? This blind old man who said he loved me until I echoed it; I was not the kind of person to leave someone like that. And who would believe I'd left him because of anything but his helplessness? So for a while I convinced myself that love was an orgy of sacrifice. I stayed on, let his hands move everywhere they wanted because it was therapeutic, because tactility was his new sight. Those old fingers have felt every cell of my skin and four or five inches into my openings. I'd come to be known by the changing of my surfaces, understood as topography, partitioned into different zones of dryness, of moisture, striations and lumps, vein bulges, hair lengths, thicknesses of nail, ribbings of calluses. What were angles became textures and densities. I began to craft myself not for eyes but for hands. I depilated constantly, abraded my skin, smoothed myself out, toned and let go muscles according to the register of touch. I was hideous to view, but I felt better than any person alive. I practiced some kind of intimacy on him, an approximation of communion, closed-eyed fingering of his empty sockets, of every reachable part. This was the best part of our association. Not the first weeks but this. We described each other, hands and words, in a vocabulary cleansed of visual reference. This was when I was not sure I was only pretending at love. We kept his empty eyes under disinfected cloth and I'd clean my fingers and reach into his orbits and he would say the kindest things about my skin. Then these kindnesses morphed, became tinged with suggestion and reprimand. Was it that he felt so helpless while I plunged into him blindly by choice? We kept ourselves pressed together but embittering until he insulted the shape of my bones. He told me of osteotic shaving. I fled when he recommended pelvic alteration. His claim was total shock, maybe not even a lie. The sun hurt my unpracticed eyes, burned the skin of my sculpted body. The drive to my parents' house was chapping and full of stares and I cried most of it.*

Ellie again recites her diary or monologue and it's true or close. Her index finger rests on one of the glass eyes, rotates it idly on the table. Her interlocutor watches, itches to touch. He's another William, Ellie's age, more ragged than the old man. She brought him over after meeting him on the internet, an act that always felt a little like conjuring. He's listening patiently like the ad said, like she'd repeated when he first got there.

*I rested and regained my visual composure in the privacy of my parents' home. Some weeks of eating properly, hiding in my childhood bed. Incremental backyard tanning, hair growth, return to a more acceptable idiom. And then I moved here, took up working again. William called and forgave me, which was more than I could forgive him for. But I let him call again and we talked, maybe once a month. Eventually I even saw him. I went back for a day to watch him die.*

The William across from her unfolds his hands from his lap and Ellie lets him reach forward. She places his index finger on the eye's pupil, flips on the contact mic on the table. It's his turn now.

The advertisement is for Williams. It runs often and the kinds of Williams who read these things all know the wording already.

The first William is the dead William. This William—the ragged, youthful William she'd lycra-ed and informed—this William is leaned over the table and pressing his weight into the glass eye. A soft groan escapes him. Ellie likes the noise of his exertion.

*You want to see the real ones?*

This William nods. They tend to when she gives them the choice. She pulls them out, lights up their case. The real eyes bob a little and string out their blood behind them. William is thinking about what it would be like to have sex with Ellie. He is. He puts the glass eye in his hand up to the glass case with the real eyes, rubs it back and forth to look into them both. Ellie tells him it's enough, unpeels his lycra, puts him back in his jeans.

This obese William can't stretch on the black body suit she needs him in. Ellie tells him to call if he slims down.

This William she wants but holds back from. He tells her the things he most desires. The list is entirely physical.

This William she meets at her bank. He'd read her ad. She takes him home and fills his mouth with glass, makes him ululate while she traces out the hole of his ear. Again. Again and others.

It isn't therapeutic and it doesn't have anything to do with her fragile psyche. Ellie's convinced herself that art is a series of heightened gestures, oversignifying and emptily erotic. One day she'll cover walls with identical eyes all ordered up to look like William's. The sounds of her recordings will fill the room with echoing screeches, oblique percussion, clipped accounts of sexual fantasy. Enter William, flattened, universal, commodity-William. William her identity and hers. William invested with meaning to sell so she can quit the bank. Isn't it neat?

The one thing she can't sell is the taste of sucking glass.

# REUNION

The kissing robot had the biggest lips in the room. They should be thinner and easier to handle. Those enormous lips make a person feel like a tiny child. You can't lock lips because it just isn't a good fit. People should know better than to make lips like those.

I told Jeffrey, "Look at that kissing robot. Look at those ridiculous lips. It's like they were afraid you might miss."

"Not everyone has your kind of aim." Jeffrey looked sharp in his blazer. We were standing near the cheeses, looking at those lips.

The reason they had the kissing robot was for the kissing booth. $5.00 a kiss. It was for charity, which actually meant it was for a new gymnasium.

Robby Goldfarb came and stood with Jeffrey and me. He did not look sharp. He looked like he was wearing his father's suit. "Would you get a load of that kissing robot. What I wouldn't give for a few minutes alone with her."

"What would you give? And also, what exactly would you do? It's a robot." Jeffrey wore disdain more naturally than anyone I knew.

Robby made an obscene gesture that lacked definite content. His eyes were wet with expectation."It isn't even a she," I said. "It's a robot."

Robby felt pressed and started talking about how the kissing robot would give great blowjobs. I had come into the night really hoping I could avoid hearing Robby Goldfarb talk about blowjobs. I speared a cube of Gouda with a toothpick and placed it on my tiny paper plate. "You don't have to be a woman to give good blowjobs." I said.

Robby thought this was hilarious. "How would you know?" He was almost laughing too hard to pull it off, but he managed to poke his tongue several times into the side of his cheek.

"You do know that kissing robots are only anthropomorphic from the shoulders up? It's not like they have genitals," said Jeffrey.

Robby insisted that they were fully anatomically correct. The kissing robot was wearing a loose-fitting evening gown. It was impossible to tell.

We kept watching the robot. There was quite a line. One of the deans didn't seem to realize that in a French kiss, the tongue does not go around but rather into the other's mouth. In any case, the robot was a hit. The new gymnasium seemed more likely by the minute.

An attendant disinfected the robot's mouth between kisses and then sprayed mint flavor to cover the disinfectant. She was cute and a few years younger than us. It made her even cuter that she was terribly bored and seemed like she might fall asleep on her feet. She kept spraying and wiping and taking money, once a minute, all night long.

Jeffrey and I tired of critiquing the kissing technique of our former classmates. We scanned the room for ex-girlfriends. They weren't hard to find. Most of them weighed double now what they did in our memories. Then again, so did we. It was more fun to watch the kissing.

Not soon enough, the evening came to an end. They played a last dance over the loudspeaker. Most of our ex-girlfriends were married. We wouldn't have asked them to dance anyways. The song wasn't even contemporary to when we went to school.

Someone dimmed the lights for the last song and the kissing booth was finally shut down. The attendant switched off her robot and disinfected it a final time. Jeffrey stood next to her while she wiped off the robot's lips. He asked her if she would like to dance and then maybe get a drink after. He told her she could decide on the drink based on how well he danced.

"I'm an excellent dancer," he said.

She took his arm and began to waltz. He took the lead gracefully. "You are an excellent dancer," said the kissing robot's attendant.

"I wouldn't have lied."

"You never know."

They danced perfectly for the remainder of the song and she agreed to accompany Jeffrey to the hotel bar.

"I just need to finish putting away Melinda."

Jeffrey looked puzzled.

"That's her name. The robot," said the robot's attendant.

"I didn't realize the robot was a she."

"I mean, look at her."

"Out of curiosity, do you mind if I peek under Melinda's dress?"

"I think I'll take a rain check on that drink."

"No, it's not...I just wanted to see if—"

"Yeah, I know. A lot of people want to fuck her. It must be those lips."

# SOMETIMES GIRLS

I saw the cow with the glass plate grazing the lawn of the university hospital. The glass plate is on the cow's side, so you can see into the cow.

Inside the cow is dark and bloody. If you shine a light at the glass plate, you can see better. You can see the organs that are in the immediate vicinity of the plate.

There is also a hinge on the plate, so you can open the cow and reach inside and find out what the inside of a cow feels like. Or at least, you can find out what the inside of the cow feels like in the area right behind the glass plate. You could if you could open the plate, but you need to know the right combination for that. The researchers keep the inside of the cow locked up.

I told Steven about the experimental cow. I told him I knew where the experimental cow lived and at which times it could be found grazing.

"We should steal that cow," he said. We stole the experimental cow.

After we stole the cow, we hid it in my basement. My backyard is on a slope, so you can get to the basement through a back door that is on ground level. That's why we chose my basement instead of Steven's. For his basement, we would have had to take the cow down a flight of stairs.

It took us a few days to figure out the combination, but eventually we unlocked the cow.

The glass plate was about a foot in diameter. It was round. Steven told me I should open the cow. Neither of us wanted to be the one to open her.

"You open her," I said.

"You open her," said Steven.

The cow was very patient. I mowed the lawn and brought her the grass clippings and she stood next to the broken treadmill and ate happily. Soon she finished the clippings, so Steven mowed his yard and we brought her those. She started mooing. I was worried the neighbors might come.

"Okay," I said. "Open her now."

Steven opened the experimental cow. Her guts slipped out of the portal and started bleeding on my carpet.

We tried to close the cow, but she just kept spilling out of herself. The more we tried to fix the situation, the more cow got onto the carpet and the less cow stayed in the cow. The glass plate was all the way open and pushed up against her side. The cow was mooing with full force now and Steven and I were totally covered in blood.

I tipped the cow over onto her side and grabbed a bucket from the garage, then I scooped all the inner-cow off my carpet and poured it back into her body. Steven slammed her window shut.

The cow kept mooing horribly. I felt sick. Steven excused himself to the bathroom. The cow was bellowing and kicking and we knew she'd die if we didn't call the researchers who built her. We also knew we'd go to jail for theft of an experimental animal.

After I called the researchers, they rushed to my house. They were furious researchers. The experimental cow was worth several million dollars. Also, she was useless for anything besides experiments. She didn't even produce proper milk.

I asked them to please forgive me. I told them, "I am very sorry."

Steven hid in my shower before the researchers came.

The researchers told me they didn't care that I was sorry. They were going to press charges because I stole their cow and nearly killed her. (Thankfully, they managed to save the cow. Some of the researchers, besides being academics, were also highly accomplished veterinarians.)

Because I didn't want to go to jail, I told them that they could experiment on me if they wanted. The researchers huddled and conferred. One of them stepped forward. He was tall and had an unfortunately shaped nose. He extended his hand and I shook it.

Anyway, I only let the researchers open the glass plate. Sometimes girls.

# THE REASON I GET SO MANY PARKING TICKETS

I wanted her to know that even though her brother arrested me, I still thought she was cute. It was something to do with her cheekbones.

She was saying to someone that she didn't really know what virginity meant because as far as she could tell, it was impossible to determine where the interior ended and the exterior began and so then how do you ever know if and when penetration has occurred? Then she saw me looking at her and asked me how come I wasn't in jail and didn't her brother arrest me and would she have to call him to arrest me now or was I over my whole thing with breaking glass?

I gave her a mostly blank but maybe slightly pouty look which was meant to signify that the thing about the breaking the beer bottle was not true and she knew that and that she also knew that I'd just been trying to clean up the bottle that Andy had broken by accident and incidentally only because her brother's friend had spilled beer on the floor and so made it a treacherous surface.

Actually I think I looked retarded. I realized and told her that I was sorry and that I realized I had just given her a retarded-looking look and she said not to say retarded. So I felt embarrassed and had to re-begin my apology-slash-explanation and explain that I had given her and then offensively labeled that look because I was trying to psychically retell the story of my arrest in order to both exonerate myself and in the process shame her into an apology.

She remained haughty and her cheeks were a little flushed. I asked her if, by her previous logic, it would be fair to say that we were kissing. She told me it was fair, but that actually the logic extended to say the whole population of the world was fucking each other at the same time all of the time and all the animals and objects too. Which is why, she said, she so strongly believed in monogamy.

We started talking about all of the fucking we were doing, like fucking the president and sea anemones, and dead Mahatma Gandhi. She was laughing and I was also laughing. I would say 'the Empire State Building!' and she would reply 'Bikini Atoll!' and I think she had a mind to ask me out, or might at least have said yes to me if I had asked.

Then her brother walked in in full uniform and his badge was on his chest and polished like a mirror and I shouted, 'Your brother!' and we both kept on laughing right at him.

# THE WRESTLING BEAR

Look at the sun gleaming off of that bear's fur. It's warming her as she sleeps. Inside of her is a cub that is tiny and hasn't yet developed any fur. Outside of her is a circular cage and a sign that invites any and all takers to come fight the bear. Winners make 100 dollars. Winning means lasting 7 minutes in the bear cage.

She is a little bit ragged and the concrete floor beneath her is cracking and starting to grow weeds. To make the fighting fair, her claws and teeth have been removed. The only thing she eats is fish and berry slop from a bucket, slurping it into her mouth with her long tongue. Her paws ache and her gums tend to bleed and the course of her bleeding leaves dry and matted streaks on her cheeks that give her a more savage appearance.

She was outside not so very long ago, and she had loveless sex with a larger and younger male bear and that is why she is pregnant. Her handler doesn't know that his bear is pregnant or even a girl. He calls her Thunder Bolt and tells people that she killed two consecutive Comanche Indian chiefs and that after that the Comanche people regarded her as a god and sacrificed their sick and weak in order to appease her anger and secure a bountiful harvest. He says that he captured her by cunning in the dead of the night and that now she fights like a demon out of her desire to eat more human flesh. Except, of course, he says 'he' when referring to her.

In fact, he caught her with a steel trap and she fights like she does because he underfeeds her and prods her with sticks to make her angry. She's sleeping now, but soon the prodding will begin and then the bravest of men will pay 20 dollars each for a chance at out-wrestling her. Her handler will make sure things don't get too out of hand and the bravest of men will leave with only a few bruises and maybe a small broken bone and 20 dollars fewer. Mostly they'll be happy to have the story of surviving even a minute or two against the bear-god Thunder Bolt.

But today she will face off against a powerful man with a huge red beard and a handlebar mustache and a faded red singlet from his college wrestling days. His wife will be wearing a pale yellow jumper and she will hold the hand of their toddler and watch as the red-bearded man hurls himself at the bear's midsection. He will not reach her though. She will catch him in her de-clawed paws and lift him swiftly above her head and hold him there. Her handler will prod and prod and try to force her to drop the man, but she will hold him up and all of his exertions will do nothing to loosen her grasp. She will wait like that until the cage is opened for the other men to try to bring her down, but she will wade through them and into the fairgrounds and she will not release the red-bearded man. She will walk with him to the Ferris wheel and cut right to the front of the line and take her seat in the little metal carriage. As the wheel takes them upward, the bear will pull the man to her chest and hold him tightly against her and wait like that to reach the wheel's highest point. Then, she knows, she will have to decide whether to jump.

# HALFINGERS

87

She took a hold of his little wet hand (a thick and difficult wet, slicked out of her), and she took him by it towards the room that was all light and fuzz.

Her mouth lipped around his fingers and softened them up with its own wet before starting in on the chewing.

# STAR CHARTING

This time my eyes stayed open the whole while. Not that I can see vibrations. Not that there were things yet to see. I kept the blinds drawn in any case, out of caution, out of courtesy.

The only thing to watch was my dog, lying there in her corner, nearly silent, vomiting from nerves. All this shaking left her a wreck.

Come morning the apartment next to mine would be a tunnel, Jeep-shaped, messy with wall plaster. As for my neighbors? Sometimes the uncertain's just best left unsaid.

*

In the sunlight I scrap-picked. My ex-neighbors had nice things: a teakettle, dishware, some kitsch figurines in ceramic. My dog nosed through the open refrigerator. I'd already eaten my fill and stashed the good condiments in an old fundraiser tote. The meat in the freezer I left out to thaw.

The tunnel had gone straight through my neighbors' living room. I sat myself in the remains of a love seat and looked down the long passageway. House after house it went on, with neighbors like me picking over each ruin.*

I was glad they'd come so close. That meant my apartment wasn't part of the pattern. It was stars, we were told. If you mapped it out, the whole city was overlapping stars.

Some friends of mine had taken up cartography. They were walking the tunnels, measuring, marking out paths against an old municipal map. They were the ones who told me about the stars. *Some firmament* I said. *More like scars* I said. The cartographers laughed a little.

They were the ones collecting all the stuffed dolls from the tunnels. Meanwhile they burned or buried every photograph they found with a face. Loss is easier to swallow when it's been depersonalized, when it can just as readily map onto universal nostalgia, to the end of childhood as easily as a disappeared person. At least that's what the cartographers thought. So they were lining a whole corridor with salvaged dolls, separating them by species and native habitat, like in a zoo. The bears were the most plentiful. And the babies.

*

I took to spending days in the baby enclosure. I'd bring batteries for the ones with motors and set them crawling. They were loud and mechanical as they labored away, down past the mass of stuffed birds, past the lightly populated reptile room.

I took my dog along for her exercise. She mouthed a little plastic head. You could hardly call it chewing.

A cartographer friend let me title myself *zookeeper*. I wanted something grander: *royal tunnel zoologist*. I had a habit of wanting grandeur. At the market, I traded my neighbors' belongings for gilded keepsakes: candlesticks mostly, and machine-wrought frames.

*

As for human touching: that had happened before, confusedly. It was a poor substitute for desire. I wouldn't read too much into my time with the zoo babies. Maybe it's just that my dog prefers their faces. The other animals are too much like her.

Unlike the cartographers, I was mostly alone here. When whole roads get carved from your neighborhoods, it's just easier not to expend care. Besides, a dog is enough life for anyone to be responsible for in a constant aftermath like this one.

And the stars themselves, I kept wondering, what were they for? I mean, we all knew what they did. We knew what they were: transit lines, life mines, symbolic geometry. One could walk them. One could line them with things or strip them of their valuables. But what something *is* is hardly the same thing as what it's *for*. And in terms of that, all I can say is that it's amazing how space can determine the contours of possibility, can smooth down or flatten out a life to its barest dimension. Or maybe what I mean is that the worst part of a catastrophe is the normalcy that settles in after.

# JELLY BODIES

The abrasion of cellular effluvia.

The pumice stone exertions.

The incantatory self-denunciation.

The barbed twine arcing and whipping (those little teeth don't so much bite as tunnel into the skin of my back).

Dermal excess piles on the floor, ablutions accrete——a wall against sin.


<*With a fine enough razor, you can skin the outer layer off your person so the blood wells up without any actual loss. Do so. Follow that with a full-body coating of petroleum jelly. Floss until your only bleeding part is your gums and then, each day, weave that blooded thread into a rust and beige quilt. Bite out the eyes with your mouth and wear the quilt as a hood.*>


A fine and shaming hood, uneven blooded streaks and patches gorging, shifting with sweat.
Teeth mirror-polished.

Scentless body, innocenting flesh.

<*What of skins? Of excess petroleum jelly? It won't do to build your wall with*

An army of witness, built of shaven skins.

Skins stuffed full of blood-stained jelly, sewn closed with excess floss.

Jumbling jelly men, jelly mess, lining the walls to watch the discarding of parts, the birth of each new model.

A jelly man packed and sent.

Ream him through or suction out his stomach.

Tattoo him with the proper names, run him over, feed his body to the stray dogs that gather some days near the southern edge of town.

This floss hood for him.

Embalming materials and a full-color set of spray paints.

This map as a regional account of his body, organized according to sin.

*<Burn your maps and know that a witness is not simply the image of a past self set to guard a fearful present. Slice your next skin into long thin strips, as if making bacon. Hickory smoke them. Mail them via Next Day Air.>*

Smoked skins in a vacuum-sealed container.

A town razoring, stuffing. A town sewing. They have taken up the practice, stuffing their shaved-off skins with excess petroleum jelly.

Jelly men, jelly women, all properly hooded, all looking skyward in the correct and humble manner.

Town full of jelly people, too many for our small houses. A barn converted for storage. Barn full of jelly bodies, piled, mounding. Jelly bodies warping flat into stuffed skin planks.

*<There must be no more jelly people. The only proper skin treatment is hickory smoke. Jelly people may become animated, dangerous. It is a matter of atmospheric conditions. Destroy the stored bodies. Pull the sides of each hood together around each jelly head so the petroleum jelly expresses in flows through the weave. Pile the bodies onto barges, set them afloat, torch upon the river. Continue skin mailings.>*

A female jelly body, Sheila Mitchell's, head crushed, breasts pressed into my face. Accidental but—and in the attempt at disposal.

Those big soft jelly breasts squeezed around and fitted to my head.

Live Sheila Mitchell saw.

Accusation of suckling, jelly-body molestation.

Vacuum-sealed bag of skins, properly crisped, but only mine.

Town has sided with Sheila Mitchell.

Skins prepared exactly as requested—pure hickory smoked to a tender consistency.

Memory of Sheila Mitchell's jelly breasts: A slight skin-tear in the left areola leaks interior jelly onto my cheek. I tongue the side of my floss hood, tasting.

Her insides mixing with petroleum jelly.

The flattened oozing hood, trails of jelly creeping down that torso. My shaved mouth interior after tasting (pink smoked strips in the vacuum bag).

Am no longer permitted near the jelly bodies.

*<Electro-chemical composition of this seasonal air likely will lead to jelly body animation within days. Burn their storage room. Torch it tonight, immediately after full darkness.*

*Shave off your skin and ball it into a spare floss hood. Douse it thoroughly in gasoline until soaked and sopping. Self-immolation is a necessary risk. Tie the bottom of the hood shut with a length of cord and tie a brick also to the same cord. Light your hood/skin wad and throw the brick full force through the window, into the storeroom of jelly bodies.*

*Follow with a bucket of gasoline, making sure to provide paths for the flames to engulf all bodies. Again, the risk of self-immolation is present but necessary.*

*Once home, razor your newest skin layer from your body, dice it, feed it into your wood-burning stove. Do not hickory smoke this layer. The gas fumes will have already ruined it.>*

The bodies burned, destroyed.

Skin discarded, burned.

One lie: Sheila Mitchell's body I saved.

I pulled it out, headless and jelly-slopping.

Am not suckling, but tasting leaked jelly (not forcing any expression).

I leave it sit on my gums, taste it long and subtle like chaw.

*<Rebuild your ablutionary wall. Collect your sloughings and leavings, stack them against the Mitchell body. Do not leave your house. Do not allow visitors to pass through your door.*

*As you insist on maintaining the body, be sure to take correct precautions:*

*On the animation night, make love to the body in purity and passion. Become in an ecstasy of true love. Inflate the body's floss hood with your breath, stitch every skin tear with sinews you pull from your bones.*

*Air currents will only maintain animation for 60 to 72 hours. Towards the end of the animation period, the body may become violent and demanding. Accommodate unless absolutely unable. Duration of animation state is largely determined by the animated body's degree of satisfaction in combination with atmospheric conditions. Preferable conditions are cool with moderate humidity. Winds, 15–20 miles per hour, blowing in a southwesterly direction, are thought to be ideal.*

*And remember your penance catalog. Scrub, razor, amass, smoke, send. Purchase a spice kit to improve smoke quality. Hickory grows old.>*

*<Report on the jelly body. Send new skins. If worrying over spices, consider cardamom.>*
*<Report on the jelly body. This passage of weeks is worrisome.>*

Following weather patterns, Sheila Mitchell's body and I have maintained the animated state.

Against recommendation, have not consummated relationship.

Body is not attracted to me physically.

Lack of intercourse has not been detrimental to animation.

Condition: Sheila Mitchell's body's head slumps, but is otherwise functional.

Floss hoods have been removed for use as fishing nets.

The fish in this river are good to eat (I will send).

Two fish, cleaned, smoked with hickory and cardamom.

# THE HAPPY-ENOUGH FAMILY ON THE DAY OF THE SORROWS-WEIGHING

That they were not working class was listed as a problem for them, something they construed as a problem in order to reach the troubles-quota that families from the region were meant to meet. On the ledger it was listed under Problems of Excessive Guilt.

A daughter also, in amounts that exceeded the normal range, was known to think about suicide. She'd even tried that trick once or twice, halfheartedly, as that particular problem counted a long way towards a family's necessary minimum of unhappiness.

This month though, their biggest problem was a meta-problem, was that they hadn't enough problems for the quota, and that didn't count as a proper Sorrow.

This month, they knew, the weight of their problems would not be enough, even wetted down, even with bits of lead slipped into the pockets.

The young one would have to take up self-harm, cutting maybe, or else some symptom of body dysmorphia. The parents would have to think about divorce or the middle one might, at the very least, affect a form of paranoia or obsessive compulsion.

Other families had catastrophes: dead sons or burned houses, botched abortions, Lou Gehrig's Disease. In this family, so much in need of problems, the oldest son was not even gay, nor were his parents homophobic.

The oldest son was, however, resourceful, and he cut out problems from the stone of the quarry. He painted FAMINE or BELOW AVERAGE GRADES or SUDDEN ONSET OF APHASIA on each block of granite and gathered them and hauled them all to the courthouse for the Measurement of Sorrows.

His stones were so heavy that his family members, who had been fasting and rending their clothes and self-consciously nurturing the development of upper-class neuroses, needed not to have worried over their moderate excess of happiness. In fact, they were found to be the most heavily troubled family in the whole town and the other families, the drug-ravaged and the homeless and the child-burying families all wept en masse for the happy-enough family.

The devastated families flooded Main Street with their tears so that the not-so-unhappy family could raft down the boulevard on an impromptu pleasure cruise in a donated army-surplus lifeboat. Irony would have one or several family members drown, pitched from the raft and weighted down with some false, stone-hewn trouble of which they were too proud to release, something like ALLERGY TO RUBBER or IRRATIONAL FEAR OF WATER. Instead the family sailed to edge of their neighborhood and drank complimentary sparkling wine, a gift from the liquor store owner, who, embarrassed of his meager list of sorrows—a failing business, cataracts, knee surgery, two obese children, a loveless marriage, an unfaithful wife— had told the now-quite-happy family that, really, it was the least he could do.

# GOLDEN YOUTH IN THE CANCER BONE GARDEN

We were raised in the cancer bone garden. I remember it as a desert place, sun-bleached and domestic. There's a different family there now; we've been gone for years.

My sisters remember it for the rough-tiled courtyard, the wheelbarrow of bone chips, springtime flowers through a spinal vase. I mostly remember the sun.

Our father was the bone artist. He laid mosaics and carved reliefs, almost exclusively scenes of the saints.

My sisters would help with the sorting when a new shipment came in. The eldest even tried her hand at carving. She cut perfect miniature horses, always from the bones of children. She built a diorama of them, a whole herd that must still stand at the garden's eastern end. My job was to sweep up the bone dust they left in their wake. Father helped me mix it into the cement he used for his mosaics.

When the sun was high, my sisters and I would lie out to tan on the white reflective surface of the bone-tiled courtyard. The cancer bones would be perfectly hot and we would not move for hours save to straw lemonade and rotate from our stomachs onto our backs.Father's saints stared blankly all around us, sister's horses stood frozen at the edge of our sight.

# THE RIDER

Room full of animals smoking cigarettes. Rabbits smoking cigarettes. Deer smoking cigarettes. Possum sipping beer through a straw.

Deer and rabbits playing cards, playing Texas hold 'em. Horses playing some variation of stud. Horses in overstuffed chairs, hind hooves crossed. Dainty. Horses in black-rimmed glasses. Dog butler on hind legs, silver platter resting on his front paw (platter full of hors d'ouvres), towel draped over bent front leg.

Walls full of mounted heads, antlers. A wall of legs, some dozen different species' worth. Legs all crowded in like sea urchin spines, like blades of grass. A perpendicular lawn of legs. Hooves and claws reaching out, ready for shaking.

Opposite, a wall of tails droops its way through several square yards.

The backyard was all tall yellowed grass, untended, gnatful and thick-aired, its edge blending from brush into forest. The old carousel works had come from a few counties over, rusted and rotted out, traced faintly by the remnants of what was once a festive veneer, likely Victorian—all painted panels of women in barely-pink dresses, sprawled on grass, parasoled.

The work was done lovingly. The gears were polished and replaced as needed, the too-gone wood knocked out in favor of fresh pine. The whole contraption was painted brightly, a fresh coat on the old designs. The carousel, clearly, had been expertly restored. Upon the pull of a lever, its antique music reel started to crank, its lights blinked into color, and the carousel began to circle.

The one-legged brother watched me watching it spin.

The dogs got donated, he said. But me and George shot most of the rest.

It was George, the other brother, the two-legged one, who brought me out here. To be fair, I'd consented to the trip. Mine was the kind of ennui that led to easy drifting, a vacant faith in absolute suggestibility.

I should be clear that by 'here' I mean this this particular ranch home, low-set and sprawling, with its wood-paneled showrooms and acres of yard. I had a business reason for being in the region: some low-tier convention—bright lights and bad carpet, a large room lined with tables staffed by smiling rivals, that heavy undercurrent of future sexual regret. I'd stashed an extra bag of sponsors' samples, a few hotel soaps, an unwanted wad of over-designed business cards from men who needed no embossing. In short, I was ready to go home.

The cab I called was George's.

The bears all posed with teeth exposed, air-pawing, clawed and vicious. The coyotes were similar, but the dogs seemed docile, resigned. A horse appeared to be frozen in the midst of some dressage. Squirrels and rabbits had been set in mid-scamper. Most common were the moose and the deer, the bucks of which, run through by the enabling steel pole, floated up and down in time with the music box waltz.

Naturally, the animals were all real. I thought of them as ridable corpses. The brothers, I imagine, employed more charitable euphemisms, words like *trophies* or *art*. George suggested I pick a mount. His brother nodded in agreement. I wanted the meanest looking corpse they'd got.

George's cab had antlers on its hood and DERMY BROS. TAXI stenciled on the side in large black sans serif letters. The seats inside had deer-pelt coverings, the skins of George's kills. George chewed a cigar that looked impossibly small in his fat-lipped, deeply plunging mouth. He had always done the bulk of the driving, even before *the accident* happened. That's what they called it, always, *the accident*, and George spoke incessantly of it, though never in great detail. In any case, I was barely in the car before he asked me if, really, I needed to go straight to the station. After the accident, his brother had been up to things, things worth seeing, certainly, things to be beside or near, things I'd find worth being with.

Aboard the carousel bear, I imagine the brothers taking potshots, riddling me with weak ammunition, the kind that's more stinging than lethal. I wonder why I picture such restraint.

I splay over the bear's back and wrap my hands around his head, eventually stuffing them into his mouth so I can hold his teeth like handlebars. His fur is coarse enough to hurt. The brothers take pictures of me with an old oversized newspaper camera, a black and flash-bulbed mechanical relic. When the carousel comes to a stop, George is standing, smiling wide with the camera cradled under his arm. His brother has turned and headed to the house.

In the dead center of the leg wall is a leg that seems not to belong. The others are furred and either hoofed or clawed. A few are feathered and taloned. Some turtle legs stand out for their thick nakedness, their broad flat feet, their generally stub-like quality.

The out-of-place leg is thinly haired and, though otherwise unclothed, is shod in Reebok. The leg belonged to the one-legged brother. Robert. The one-legged brother's name is Robert. The leg still belongs to him, I guess, but in a different way than it once did. It belongs to him now as property, whereas my legs belong to me as legs.

Directly across from the leg wall is the tail wall, and between them are the taxidermy dioramas. Robert stands with his crutch in the midst of the animal bodies. George lays his big hands down on my shoulders. He says he knows I must feel that I've woken into some kind of dream. George's breath is bulking onto me. It's sticking thickly to my neck.

None of us make love, though I believe we imagine the possibility. Robert strikes the glass eye of a stuffed doe with his fingernail and draws a knife from his pocket. False eyes make for poor witnesses, he says. He doesn't smile when he says it, but his teeth are showing anyway; his lips drawn back.

I picture the sorts of grizzly things one pictures in such circumstances, endings and entrails, the effects more than their causes. No violence transpires. Robert re-pockets his knife.

George takes my shoulders and guides me out of the showroom, back past the carousel, finally into his cab. He asks me if it all made an impression and I tell him that I can't imagine it won't. George starts up his car and turns off the meter. An hour later I'm waiting for my train.

On the platform I feel his hand again on back. I turn and his other hand extends toward my chest, palm up and open. He's offering me the body of a squirrel. I take the proffered body. George tells me it's a token, a souvenir. He asks me for my business card and I hand it to him and then we wait together, in silence, his hand pressed onto me, until my train pulls in and I climb away.

A year passes in the more or less unremarkable way that years tend to pass—overfilled with small calamities, events that amass to nothing of note. And then I receive a large manila envelope in my office mail. Inside are three cassette tapes. There is nothing else in the package, nor is the envelope marked with a return address.

When I find a cassette player (the search for which constitutes a two-day non-adventure of its own), I proceed to play the first tape. What I hear is muffled but familiar speech. The voice is mine; the recordings are of nothing but me holding up my end of boring recent conversations. Tapes two and three are similar.

There is nothing threatening in the tapes, nothing embarrassing. The most disconcerting thing about them is the degraded quality of the recordings, the unpleasant sound of my voice, so vulnerably thin in that coat of hiss. I listen to the tapes a few times over, just to be sure, but they're wholly unincriminating, even dull. In any case, it can't be blackmail—there aren't any demands.

So, I wonder, then why? Is it a proof of power? A greeting card from the surveillance state? Because it seems the thing to do, I rifle through my files, check the undersides of furniture, the dark places in my plants. Eventually I do find it.

The recorder sits in the body of my dead squirrel. I pinch open his mouth to speak directly into the microphone. At first I think I'll give the brothers a message, a threat maybe, something to make them know I'm onto them before I smash up their carcass-machine. But then I think the better of it. I nestle that squirrel in my jacket pocket, beside the fountain pen, where he seems to best belong.

# ACKNOWLEDGEMENTS

---

*Pool Party Trap Loop* was originally published by Queen's Ferry Press, and it would not be the same book without the kind and thoughtful editing it received in that process.

Many of the stories in this collection were previously published, often in substantially different forms. I would like to thank the editors who helped shape and share these stories. The following stories appeared, in some version, previously. The original publications are listed in parentheses. In some cases, more than one publication published versions of a story.

Window/Screens (Noo Journal), I Would Kiss Him Back All Over Too (elimae), Planters (Digital Hamper), A Room That Is and Or Is Not Past Tense (PANK), Today for Jowled Marcus! (Digital Hamper), The Pork Shunter's Fingers (Eyeshot), Youth and Beauty (Abjective), Mother Tongue (Lies/Isle), Maldoror, Suffering From Kidney Failure, Tapes his Weekly Television Program (Lies/Isle), Dead Kids (Mad Hat Lit), Childpainter (Matchbox), GUMBOY (Puerto del Sol), You Are Today a Man (Big Lucks), EXERCISES (Tarpaulin Sky), Me, I'm Looking Out (Mud Luscious Online Quarterly), Can You Call a Ghost Your Girlfriend If She Won't Say Yes? (Kitty Snacks), Mrs. Van Pelt's Class Is Not Coming to the Assembly (Corduroy Mtn.), The Future of Dogfighting in America (Gigantic), Story of Eyes (The Collagist), Reunion (Why Vandalism?), Sometimes Girls (Dogmatika), The Reason I Get So Many Parking Tickets (Deep Leap), The Wrestling Bear (Wigleaf), Halfingers (elimae), Star Charting (El Aleph), Jelly Bodies (Lamination Colony, 5Trope),

The Happy-Enough Family on the Day of the Sorrows-Weighing (Tin House) Golden Youth in the Cancer Bone Garden (Dark Sky Magazine)

Additionally, The Pork Shunter's Fingers and Youth and Beauty were originally published by Publishing Genius as part of the e-chapbook *Science Fiction Pornography:*

I'd like to thank all those who have read and advised me on these stories and this collection, particularly Stephen Paul Martin, whose help was critical in assembling a mess of disparate stories into something more properly resembling a book.

I'd also like to thank Feliz Lucia Molina for sticking with me and Scott Spencer Jackson for his endless desire for pools by which to party.

# ABOUT THE AUTHOR

**Ben Segal** is the author of *Pool Party Trap Loop* and *78 Stories*, co-author of *The Wes Letters*, and co-editor of the *Official Catalog of the Library of Potential Literature*. His short fiction has been published by the Georgia Review, Tin House, Tarpaulin Sky, and Puerto del Sol, among others. He holds a BA from Hampshire College, MFA from UCSD, and JD from the University of Chicago. He currently lives in Los Angeles.

# Also available from NEURONICS

**Mineral Planet** – James Pate
**Interrogating the Eye** – M. Forajter
**The Selected Poems of Charles Tomás** –
translated by Carlos Lara and Tamas Panitz
**Book of Losses** – Joseph Turrent
**KRV** – Oli Johns
**Sorcererer** – Jace Brittain
**Sonnet Cycle** – Tom Will
**Burton's Anatomy** – Ansgar Allen
**Fall Garment** – Paul Cunningham
**The Isotope of I** – Connor Fisher
**The Reading Room** – Ansgar Allen
**You Alive Home Yet?** – Daniel Beauregard
**The Reaches** – Ansgar Allen
**> Get Back to Work** – Jim Redmond
**Everjescence** – Tyson Bley
**Work is Hard Vore** – Philip Sorenson
**Vagabond** – Joshua Martin
**The –Tempered Mid·Riff** – Brad Baumgartner
**I Get Groceries** – RC Miller
**Lynx Perpetual Lynx** – Colin Post
**Wretch** – Ansgar Allen
**A Large Retailer** – RC Miller
**Spelunker** – Mike Corrao
**Gynophobia** – Tyson Bley
**Normal Service Will Resume Shortly** – Tyson Bley
**Cyclops** – Tyson Bley
**Demon Drawings** – RC Miller
**Dark Poems** – Tyson Bley
**Frankencop** – Tyson Bley
**Celestial Chimp** – Tyson Bley

# Also available from SCHISM²

**Tractatus** – Róbert Gál
**Subconscious Colossus** – Carlos Lara
**Slow Hot** – Andy Choi
**Snuff Memories** – David Roden
**An Ideal For Living** – Eugene Thacker
**The Autobiography of Leisure** – Narco Pastel
**The House of the Tree of Sores** – Paul Cunningham
**Left Hand** – Paul Curran
**Coma Crossing: Collected Poems** – Roger Gilbert-Lecomte, translated by David Ball
**A Slow Boiling Beach** – Rauan Klassnik
**Serial Kitsch** – Gary J. Shipley
**Sacer** – Nicola Masciandaro
**Amygdalatropolis** – B. R. Yeager
**All the Messiahs** – Anonymous
**Thank You, Steel China** – Sean Kilpatrick
**Crypt(o)spasm** – Gary J. Shipley
**O Gory Baby** – Brad Liening
**Squeal for Joy** – David F. Hoenigman
**Pussy Guerilla Face Banana Fuck Nut** – RC Miller
**Spooky Plan** – Drew Kalbach
**Vital Signs** – Tyson Bley
**Mask With Sausage** – RC Miller
**Death Salad** – Brad Liening
**Drive-Thru Zoo** – Tyson Bley
**Necrology** – Gary J. Shipley & Kenji Siratori

SCHISM